INSANE, BUT NOT DAFT.

Mental illness has always been a taboo subject and the old asylums, like the Deva Hospital, were institutions that society demanded, but wished to forget.

The author writes with authority, a blend of fact and fiction, an insight into the problems endured by staff behind the locked doors, and the despair of patients without hope, incarcerated in the 'system', cared for but stripped of their dignity and, inevitably, their will to ever lead a normal life.

One such patient was Charlie, an unfortunate victim of circumstances, whose story is typical of what went on. Should he have been committed in the first place? Would he ever get out, or was he destined to be just another statistic...out of sight, out of mind?

A highly personal story, poignant and occasionally disturbing, INSANE, BUT NOT DAFT also serves as an invaluable record...an unofficial account, but nonetheless thought-provoking.

Stan Murphy commenced his nursing career sixty years ago in 1959 at the Deva Hospital,

in Chester, and has delved into his experience
to pen this fascinating book.

Chapter One.

It was a cold, early April morning in 1959
when I cycled to my first, and what was to be
my only full-time employment. I had never
intended to become a nurse, a policeman or a
soldier perhaps, but never a male nurse. Yet
here I was cycling to the local mental hospital
in Chester, the 'Deva', to start my first day. I
was apprehensive and my nervousness made
me shudder, so I pushed the pedals harder as I
still had three miles to travel and I did not
want to be late.

As I arrived, I inadvertently looked for the
gates that my school friends, shocked at my
choice of career, had jested about. They had
laughed and told their mates that I was going
to be the man in the white coat, the one who
came to get you when you were mad.

'We'll come and open the gates for you,' they
had mockingly said on my last day at school.
But there were no gates, just a long drive lined
with magnificent trees, neat flowerbeds, and
well-manicured lawns. I knew this anyway as I
had already attended an interview in this large,
imposing, Victorian institution. It had been a

strange experience, like visiting a small town, with its shops, laundry, church, and two farms. All these facilities were maintained by the Deva's own workforce, and yet there had been a sense of unreality about the place. It was like nothing I had imagined.

After my interview and medical I had been taken to a large main hall where a film show was being shown in front of rows of strange looking people. The men were sitting on the left side of the hall and the women were on the right. Some appeared rigid, not moving at all, while others rocked up and down, with their head in their hands. It had all seemed very strange to me.

One patient had jumped up, shouted 'God save the Queen' and then stood rigid and saluted. This had given me quite a fright and I had been relieved when the patient, following a word from a burly male nurse, had resumed his seat. As I stood at the back of this large, darkened hall I had also noticed that a nurse followed patients to the toilet...a precaution apparently to ensure they always returned! All this had overwhelmed me as I was only fifteen and I hadn't had much experience of life away from my home environment. I later realised that being a potential recruit I had been taken to the hall in order to test my reaction as part of the interview process. I did nearly change my mind and I certainly didn't intend to stay. At the main entrance on that first morning I was met by a tall, smartly dressed man who introduced himself as Mr Lawson, an assistant chief male nurse, who informed me of my hours of duty etc, and issued me with a large silver pass-key. I was instructed to collect the key from outside his office each morning when I signed in for duty. However, given the security implications if a pass-key was to get into the hands of a difficult patient, I was warned it would be instant dismissal if I lost it!

My first duties were in a ward situated at the end of an extremely long, poorly-lit corridor. The walls were made of red and yellow glazed bricks, with the occasional door, or passageway leading to the wards, or grounds. I was amazed to see the corridors full of people, walking up and down, and I wasn't sure who were patients, and who were the staff.
"You will never forget this walk," I was told by

my escort, a middle aged male nurse as we
passed signs for M.4, then M.8, and M.2; the
Tailors, Upholsterer and Barbers shop. I also
noticed that there were no female wards in this
area of the hospital, and was told that the male,
and female sides were segregated and run by
two separate administrations.
The matron was in charge of the female side,
and the chief male nurse the men's side.
The sign which intrigued me the most though
was one that stated:
'No Cycling along the Corridor'.
I couldn't imagine anyone riding a bike down a
hospital corridor, but later learned that some of
the night charge nurses did their ward rounds
on a bicycle, as there was such a long way for
them to walk.
At the end of the corridor my escort unlocked
a door and I was taken into a dormitory where
cadet nurses were making beds.
Cadet nurses aged between fifteen and
eighteen, were employed under a scheme
introduced in August 1954, to recruit young
people and prepare them for a career in mental
nursing. They were employed in various
hospital departments for periods of up to three

months, attended the local college of further education, and assisted in simple nursing tasks, such as bed-making on some of the long-stay wards. Each day at 9am and after lunch, the male cadets were also required to do an hour's physical training.

There were two large dormitories in the ward, both full of tightly packed beds, perhaps up to thirty in each. The smell immediately hit me. It was putrid, a mixture of urine, body odour, and stale smoke, and it took my breath away, though I knew that I would have to get used to it.

My new colleagues looked up and were introduced as Brian, Roy, and John. The other cadets were working in another ward and the girls were on female wards. Nobody spoke direct to me at first; they just stared at my thin, small frame, and joked how the physical training instructor, who they referred to as the 'boss', would soon build me up and turn me into a man.

I was shown how to make the beds with envelope corners.

'Don't change the sheets unless they're wet.

There's not enough linen,' Roy had said.
The beds were so tightly packed that they
touched the back of my legs when I bent over
to make the next one. I also couldn't believe
what I was seeing; some of the beds were wet
and dirty, from body excretions, and other
unidentifiable stains. There was soil, cigarette
ends and the odd insect, usually a cockroach.
Then there was what I was told were the
patients' private treasures, hidden in pillow-
cases and under mattresses. There were
cigarette tins, papers, pennies, and sweets and
one cadet said they had even found a live
wood-pigeon under one of the pillows.
I asked where all the patients were and was
told they were locked up in the main part of
the ward. I hadn't realised how big some of
these wards were, or how extensive the
hospital grounds were. It was really all so
strange and I was certain, after seeing so many
dirty beds, that I would leave before the day
was over. However, I cheered up when we all
went off to the gymnasium.
The physical training instructor, ex-army, met
us in the grounds. He looked like I expected all
gymnasts to look...fit and muscular and with a

certain swagger. As he walked towards us his arms were slightly flexed and his stomach muscles were pulled in, as if he wanted to impress his authority on me, the new boy.

'Get yours hands out of your pockets,' was the first thing he said.

He looked at me dismissively.

'Not another,' he added, apparently alluding to the size of my physique. He then inquired into my sporting attributes and did I play football? I told him that I could, but later found out that I couldn't...well not good enough to play regularly for the hospital staff team. He said, rather surprisingly, that I could play for the patients' team.

My first hour at the gym was spent scraping mud off football boots and sorting out the dirty kit from the previous Saturday's match. At the same time I listened to fascinating tales from my new colleagues as they bragged about girlfriends won and lost during the weekend. The conversation quickly changed to the match and those players not present were criticised for the defeat.

I was informed of the activities cadets were expected to undertake during their daily two-hour P.T. sessions. As well as keeping the gymnasium and the equipment clean, there was football, cricket, basketball, weight training, and gymnastics. There was a sport I hadn't heard about, 'shinty'. This, I was told, was like hockey, but much rougher and more competitive.

The codes of discipline were also explained to me. I was told that if I was cheeky, caught drinking, or late for work, I would have to do 'jankers' instead of P.T. This was the first stage of punishment and it meant being sent during the P.T. sessions to the chief male nurse's office where miscreants had to rule lines in books, or run messages. It sounded like being back at school.

I soon found out that the afternoon session was badly timed as it followed lunch. The meals were free to staff below the age of eighteen and so the cadets always ate too much, which was hardly conducive to participating in strenuous exercise afterwards.

The 'boss' was a fair-minded man and treated every body the same, even though he did push me at first, obviously in an endeavour to get me fitter and stronger. During the first few weeks, I hardly had the energy to cycle home and often fell asleep straight after my tea. Sometimes the 'boss' would have to exert his authority, especially when one of the cadets got too cocky, or didn't pull their weight with the rest of the 'team'. The younger ones he would threaten, but to the bigger, older, lads he he would issue a challenge.

'Come down to the gym and put the gloves on,' was a sufficient threat to keep everyone under control.

I soon found out that the discipline was strict, almost regimental, with daily inspections of work and appearance. As the new boy I was the last in the pecking order, so I was expected to do all the fetching and carrying, until someone else started, of course. The senior cadet seemed to have more power than the prefects had enjoyed at school and we juniors were 'disciplined' for the slightest misdemeanour's. Life was not all fun and a good deal of bullying went on.

All male cadets wore uniform, three piece suits, and always looked very smart, mainly due to another more rigorous weekly inspection by one of the three assistant chief

male nurses. I was measured up by the hospital
tailor for my suit, which included a waistcoat,
something I hadn't worn before. I found the
tailor sitting cross-legged on his bench, sewing
away. He gave me a second-hand, navy blue
suit which was made of thick, coarse material.
It was too big and the trousers chapped my
legs.

'That will do you until your own suit is ready,'
said the tailor and off I went to my first
allocation, the barber's shop which was
situated halfway down the main corridor, next
to the chief male nurse's office and a ward,
Male Four (M4).

I knocked on the door, entered, and saw a
small man sitting in a barber's chair. He was
reading a newspaper, and introduced himself
as Mr Hurst, the barber. He said that staff were
no use on the wards unless they could shave
the patients and cut their hair. That was why
the Barber's shop was the first placement for
cadets as we had to master the skills. Other
placements were to include the Pathological
Laboratory, Pharmacy, Tailor's shop, Kitchen's
and Gymnasium. The prestigious allocation
was the hospital secretary's office where you

would mix with the bosses...and take the hospital secretary's dog, 'Pip', for a walk.

The barber was about five feet tall, middle-aged, and like most barbers he enjoyed talking to his customers, repeating the same stories to all and sundry.

There were two chairs in the salon, one for him and one for his 'apprentice' which on this occasion was me. His first customer on most days was a patient named Wilf, a long-stay patient with not much hair. Every morning the barber would massage Wilf's scalp with a secret solution he kept in a vinegar bottle. Hair restorer, it was supposed to be.

The barber would shake this mixture on to Wilf's scalp and massage it in with vigour, and sure enough, each day they found a new hair growing, an event greeted with delight. I was encouraged to join in with these daily celebrations although Wilf still looked as bald as a coot to me.

Outside the barber's shop was a traditional red and white pole, which seemed appropriate, considering the amount of blood I had shed during my first few shaves. I hadn't even started shaving myself, more than once a week. My first task was lathering the patients' faces with soap, using a large shaving brush. 'Work it in, using circular motions, pull the nose up, to soap over the top lip,' the barber instructed me. I lathered my first patient for what seemed like hours. I wish he'd stop talking and come and shave this poor soul, I thought.

My first shave was a bloodbath.

'You're not stretching the skin enough when you shave,' the barber explained. 'Be more careful in future. Put a wet towel over his face, then use the septic pencil on his cuts'.

After a fortnight I was introduced to the art of hair-cutting. I had become quite expert at shaving, especially when the patient kept still. One patient in particular used to gradually slide down the chair and we were both practically on the floor, when I had finished. Hair-cutting was fairly successful at first as cadets always practised on the older, balding patients, who were nearly scalped before they came in. Many had their hair cut by the nurses on the ward, but some still liked to visit the barber's shop.

One morning a patient called Don came in for

a trim. He was over six feet tall and built like a tank. The barber, who always liked to peep and see who was waiting outside, whispered to me that Don was trouble. He was rarely let out on his own and had the reputation for needing six nurses to handle him when he went 'up the pole'. This really filled me with confidence. 'Don't worry son,' said the barber, 'he must be good mood, or he wouldn't be here. You can cut his hair today, it will be good experience for you.'

Don entered, looked around, and then sat down in my chair. He wore his hair like Elvis Presley, i.e. thick, jet-black, greased, with a quiff in the front. It was his pride and joy. He sat in the chair, moodily starring at me in the mirror, while the barber sucked up to him with small talk. I thought he would take over, but he said,

'Get on with it son.'

I kept combing his hair as I was unable to get started because my hands were trembling so much. When I did finally turn on the clippers, they somehow ran up the back of Don's head, like a lawn mower cutting through long grass, leaving a path up the back of his head.

The barber nearly had apoplexy, and spent the next half hour trying to repair the damage, joking and cajoling Don as he sat fidgeting in the chair.
I spent the rest of the day brushing up hair, mostly Don's.

Chapter Two.

Charlie woke up disorientated. 'Where am I?' he asked himself, confused and frightened by his inability to remember where he was, and how he had got there.

The room was dark and featureless. He could not feel any objects in the dark and there was an awful smell of urine. He later found out he had been thrown into a padded call, closely followed by a rubber pot to wee in.

The padded cell was a windowless, dark room, about 10 x 8 feet. All the walls and the floor were padded and the floor rose slightly in the middle. A small gutter ran around the sides, allowing any urine from patients who wet themselves, or spillage from their pot, to drain into a small grid in the corner.

A dim light was fixed into the wall, covered by unbreakable glass, with the switch on the outside of the door. There were two doors, an inner thick and padded one, with a peep-hole, which was locked by two large brass bolts, and an outer door, which matched the other doors in the ward and gave a sense of normality. This too had a peep-hole and lock.

Charlie had no idea how long he had been there. He felt very drowsy and was thirsty. By the taste in his mouth, the smell in his nostrils, and the pain in his buttocks, he soon began to realise, from previous experience, that he had been given an injection of paraldehyde, probably 10ccs. This was the standard practice when the 'heavy gang' had been required to quell violent or disruptive behaviour.

Charlie's crime had been to assault a psychologist while being assessed. This was his third time in the pads and so he was now confined to the ward and would again lose his parole, his access to the grounds, shop, and other activities.

Charlie came to this place, this mental hospital, five years ago, in the spring of 1959. He was eighteen and came from a disturbed family environment. He had a history of disruptive and unpredictable behaviour. Not madness, as they said it was, but he knew he was prone to violent behaviour, from the least provocation, and sometimes without it.

The events leading up to him being 'put away' were that he had reacted violently to an incident outside his house, where he lived with his mother, brothers and sisters. He had the street in uproar, for the umpteenth occasion, and later smashed up the house. He had then gone out, ended up in a pub, only to return in a drunken state. Locked out, he had attempted to climb in through a bedroom window, but only succeeded in getting himself stuck. His sister, whose room he had been trying to enter, had screamed 'blue murder' and his mother expecting his return, had come rushing in and started beating him about the head with a coat hanger.

The police were called and to the delight of his neighbours who had been woken up by the commotion, Charlie was hauled off in a waiting police van. The police took him to the local asylum and the staff were warned that he was violent, uncontrollable and mad.

His mother and his G.P. had threatened him with this course of action on many occasions, but he had never taken them seriously as he did not have the insight, or the disposition for that matter, to appreciate that his action were not acceptable.

He had got worse after leaving school and started drinking. He had once worked as an apprentice, to a painter and decorator, but had refused to get up on time, so lost his job and was on the dole.

Bored and broke he had nobody to guide him through life and his family wanted him out of the house. The family doctor, who had never been too sympathetic to his cause had agreed to have him certified.

Later this classification would be changed to a section of the new Mental Health Act of 1959, which was being introduced that year.

Charlie sobered up considerably on his short journey to the asylum and was sore all over from the way he had been unceremoniously dragged off, and thrown roughly into the police van. The thought had crossed his mind that they appeared more psychotic than him.

He was taken to the admission ward, situated at the back of the hospital. Where the 'reception' committee met him. One of the welcoming party really stood out; he was just over five feet tall, but powerfully built...and had taken his shirt off in readiness for his arrival.

Charlie was hauled through the door by the police, and approached by the big hairy man.

He wanted to be sick, but was grabbed by numerous hands and pinned to the floor while the handcuffs were removed.

He heard the big fellow, who was apparently nicknamed 'Slim', and in charge of the hospital that night, say that this was a taste of what he would get if he didn't behave himself.

Charlie was given an injection of paraldehyde, a hypnotic, half of it injected into each of his buttocks. While this was being administered one nurse pressed his knees into the back of Charlie's legs to prevent him moving them, whilst a forearm, into the back of his neck, kept him held down.

This was the first acquaintance with a padded cell and the final indignity of the night was to be hit on the back of the head with the black piss pot that followed him in.

The next day Charlie was taken out of the 'pads' and allocated a bed at the bottom of the dormitory. He was bathed, and his height and weight taken, which was recorded with details of his general appearance. This was the usual procedure for all new admissions, and necessary information in case the patient escaped.

A male nurse recorded any marks or bruises which were visible on his body. He was black and blue due to the previous night's activities, but soon learned that such marks were merely attributed to 'falls and accidents'.

Sitting up in bed, he surveyed his surroundings. He was in a large dormitory, with two rows of beds. Six, including his own, were occupied, the furthest being at the top of the dormitory where the occupant snored loudly, obviously sleeping off his medication. Those in the other four beds had got up, but were kept in their pyjamas. There was a large fire grate at the bottom of the dormitory, with side rooms and the pads on either side. The fire was protected by a locked fire-guard.

The beds were allocated according to the level of observation each patient required. New admissions, suicidal risks, or patients with unpredictable behaviour, slept at the bottom of the dormitory, where a male nurse was always on duty, and the staff took it in turns to keep those patients under constant observation. They were not allowed to get out of bed without the nurse's permission, or put their heads under the blankets. They were accompanied to the toilet.

It was custom and practice to be kept in bed for up to a week, and sometimes then they would only be allowed to wear dressing gowns and pyjamas. Charlie, when allowed to get dressed, was made to wear old-fashioned clothes which were too small for him and not to his own stylish liking. He was very distressed and disorientated for several days. He remembered being drowsy, slept a lot, and was always thirsty. He used to put his mouth under the tap when being escorted to the toilet, gulping down water, but being unable to quench his insatiable thirst. He was also very frightened, alarmed and petrified at the behaviour of some of his fellow patients, and was also wary of some of the staff, who were strict and not sympathetic to his plight. His drowsiness was due to his medication which was given three times a day, and at night. It was normally in tablet form, but any refusal or reluctance to take it was met by an injection of what was known as P.R.N medication. (P.R.N. Pro re nata, meaning as the occasion arises.) This meant that it could be given at the discretion of the nurse in charge, and could be a traumatic experience, often followed by a long sleep.

The day started early, as the lights went on at 6am, and the patients were aroused from their beds, and sent to the wash room. Charlie was allowed to wash and shave himself with a locked razor, under the watchful eye of a nurse. The emphasis was always on safety from self-harm and there were no chains in the toilets and the bath taps had keys. The water was let out by the staff who operated a foot pedal situated on the outside of the bath. Following their toileting, most patients were encouraged to make their own beds before going to the day room for their breakfast. The food was good and plentiful, with a choice of cereals and a cooked meal. One of the patients, waiting to be moved to a long stay ward, told Charlie that a roof over his head, and three meals a day, was more than he had outside, so he was content to stay, especially during the winter months.

The mixture of people on this ward was remarkable. There was the suicidal, the violent, the down and outs, the tramps and the general unfortunates. Charlie, who was getting more paranoid each day, counted himself as being one of the latter as he had been admitted under circumstances beyond his control and branded mentally ill, without the right of a proper appeal. Not to be believed or heard, he told his table mates.

After a few days, the shock of his current predicament began to sink in and Charlie's thoughts became more irrational. His mood began to change from apathy to anger and then depression and hopelessness. Consequently, his behaviour also changed. It alternated from verbal aggression to black moods and weeping. And to further heighten his despair, he found thoughts of 'ending it all' creeping into his head. In his lucid moments he didn't think he was suicidal, but he couldn't think of anything else that would get him away from this place. He was vaguely aware that his behaviour was substantiating the belief of the doctors and nurses that he was mentally ill. Conversation with his peers was difficult, but Charlie did find himself becoming friendly with one of the patients who sat at the same meal table.

This patient appeared to have some insight

into his illness and was able to express his views and opinion of Charlie's situation which he declared was not good.

His name was Edward. He had been admitted to the hospital on several occasions, sometimes as a voluntary patient and sometimes against his will, when he had no insight that he had become ill again.

Charlie thought him lucky in many respects, as his wife and family had always supported him and he was able to return home when his symptoms abated. He said that his family, having insight into his mood swings, saw to it that he was admitted, even though he was not always agreeable, so his remissions were often caught early and were treated.

Charlie was shocked and surprised at Edward's insight and what he was capable of doing when he was ill. He confided in Charlie that he heard voices that told him to do awful things, both to himself and others. He had beaten up his wife, set fire to the house and threatened his neighbours. When this happened, he had little awareness of his actions and had lost his dignity and self-respect. This had caused awful problems for the rest of the family with their neighbours and friends. Things had become so bad that he was now worried about how much more his wife could take, and he truly had a Jekyll and Hyde personality. He said he cried for days when well enough to be told of these dreadful acts he had allegedly committed. Charlie cooled his relationship with Edward on hearing these daily accounts of his illness and he soon found himself unable to trust him with his own thoughts and feelings.

Charlie also found out that there was a pecking order amongst the patients on the ward, and their attitude towards him, and each other, was very intimidating. They had their own little areas within the ward, their own routines, and their own chairs which sometimes led to fights, if the confused or unknowing sat in them.

The staff respected this order of things to some degree. It kept the ward quiet. The higher profile patients were given larger meals, had a choice of activities and were first in the queue to use the snooker table, or have a bath.

Some patients were called 'trustees' and ran messages for some of the patients and staff. The trustees also helped with general duties on the ward, including shaving and serving meals. Others assisted in basic work that was necessary to run the hospital. Their reward was payments by cash, tobacco, sweets or special privileges.

One trustee on Charlie's ward was a man called Arthur who was also the 'kitchen man'. He was in a powerful position as far as most of the patients were concerned. He was allowed to control who had what...the little extras, such as cups of tea and an extra round of toast. Charlie soon realised that to gain his favour would be to his advantage for although it sounded petty in his current predicament, an 'unofficial' cup of tea was a God-send. After a few weeks on the ward, Charlie himself volunteered to assist in general ward duties and saved, or stole, cigarettes and tobacco to gain Arthur's favour. Another thing he learned was that Arthur was also the staff's eyes and ears and reported everything he saw. He sometimes made things up to get other patients into trouble as he himself was suspicious and vindictive. He even reported staff to the charge nurse for pinching from the kitchen, or other indiscretions.

Charlie soon began to realise how the ward dynamics worked. Some days he could actually feel the tensions in the air and this was the most dangerous times. Sometimes a patient would 'blow up' and had to be restrained and Charlie knew if he was in the wrong place at the wrong time, he too could end up in a 'rough house', caught up in an unpleasant situation which was out of his control. So on these days he would hang around in the 'backs' (toilet area) until things cooled down.

It amazed him how quickly he let himself slip into an acceptable routine.

He thought it was partly due to the medication he was on and partly due to his apathy as he was upset at not having received visitors since his admission.

He was told that families were sometimes advised to let patients settle down before visiting. Others kept away because of the stigma of patients being there, and sometimes they simply disowned them.

Charlie thought that there appeared to be two extremes. Patients were either forgotten, vanished from the face of the earth, or extreme loyalty and concern was displayed. In the latter cases, frail and elderly relatives would often travel for hours, needing to take several buses to get to the hospital. They brought with them 'extra comforts', such as sweets, cigarettes, news, and something they required most of all...their love.

The corridors to the male wards.

Chapter three.

Following my three months stay in the Barber's shop where I had eventually gained some of the skills in the art of hairdressing, I moved to my next allocation, the Pathology Laboratory. This was a more technical environment with a staff of three, i.e. the senior pathologist, a lab technician and a syringe department orderly. The latter was responsible, for the syringe department tucked away in the corner of the lab, for sterilising the needles and syringes.

The cadet's first duties were to assist with cleaning and sterilising equipment. Later we were taught how to do simple blood tests such as E.S.R.s, (Erythrocyte sedimentation rates) and haemoglobins. They could then move on to the more technical procedures, according to their ability. I was asked to stay for an extra three months to cover the holiday period and became proficient in doing a lot of tests.

My keenness to learn helped me develop a good relationship with the laboratory staff who taught me a great deal about pathology and I was soon allowed to do simple blood and urine tests.

I did, however, encounter problems with the syringe department orderly, a Mr Carber. He was a tubby, little man and walked with a shuffling gait. He looked very much how I imagined Mr Pickwick to be, and he even wore half-mooned glasses which he peered over. He spoke with a pseudo American accent, and always carried a brief case and came to work in a pin-striped suit that seemed so out of place.

The first time he was curt with me was when I answered the telephone when the senior staff were out on the lunch break. The caller had asked for a Dr Carber and when I replied there was no Dr Carber I was suddenly pushed aside and the phone was grabbed from my hand. Listening to the ensuing conversation, I realised that Mr Carber was calling himself 'Doctor'.

These calls were frequent, occurring at lunchtime, and it soon became a battle of wits as to who would answer the phone first when it rang. I privately thought that he must have been posing as a doctor, as he often went to town by taxi, wearing his white coat, which was unusual for an orderly. The other staff ignored him and seemed unconcerned about his behaviour, treating him as eccentric.

One day, much to my surprise, Mr Carber asked me where I planned to take my summer holidays. I told him that I had made no plans but on returning to work the next day I was astonished to find that he had arranged for me to go and stay with the hospital priests brother in Bray, Eire. I was annoyed that he had done this without my consent and, at first, I refused to go, but his personality won the day.

A few weeks later, I found myself catching the night train from Chester to Holyhead, with the address of a boarding house where he told me I was expected.

Although I had been abroad on a school trip I had not been much further than Rhyl on my own and so I was apprehensive. I arrived at Holyhead, in the early hours of the morning, boarded the ferry and went below to find the lounge bar. This was noisy and smoky, so I bought a drink, found a corner to settle down in, and eventually fell asleep. I woke up with a start thinking I was in Ireland, only to find that the sailing had been delayed due to fog and the ferry was only just leaving Holyhead.

I eventually arrived in Dun Laoghaire and caught a quaint old train to Dublin, then a bus to Bray. The bus was crowded, and the passengers were tightly cramped together with shopping. They all seemed to know each other, and I felt that with my accent I stuck out like a sore thumb. When I purchased my ticket, everyone seemed to turn around and look at me. I became more uncomfortable sitting on the bus as it slowly made its way to Bray as every time it passed a Roman Catholic Church, or a shrine, the passengers crossed themselves. At first I felt embarrassed and then I decided to cross myself now and again, but this only made me feel worse as I wasn't a Catholic, although my father had been. I simply had no idea of the troubles, or even the sectarian differences.

Thankfully, the bus finally arrived at Bray. I got off in the middle of the town and sought out my lodgings, looking forward to a meal and a much needed rest. The address I was looking for was just around the corner from the bus stop. I knocked on the door of the boarding house but was dismayed to discover that no one had heard of me. They vaguely remembered a Mr Carber, but realising my plight, kindly suggested that I share a room with three Belfast lads. This meant sharing a bed with one of them and although aghast with this suggestion, I agreed. I was too tired and dejected to do anything else.

Bray is a beautiful seaside town, surrounded by hills, with a large cross on the top of one of them. I loved the place immediately and sat for quite a while staring out to sea. Eventually I went back to the boarding house and to bed, only to be awoken suddenly in the middle of the night, by a chorus of loud snores. I became aware of a big smelly body next to me. My new room-mates had obviously been warned not to wake me. My bed mate stank of drink. I never slept again that night and when they got up they did not seem the least bothered by my presence. In fact, they were very friendly and on some days took me out with them, chatting up the girls working in Woolworth's or going to a bar for a pint. My only problem was that I found it hard to understand what they were saying as they spoke so fast.

The breakfasts were enormous and the

landlady expected us to eat everything that was on our plates. I was not encouraged to stay in the house during the day so I explored the surrounding countryside.

I visited Dublin, several times, once watching a classical car race in Phoenix Park; I climbed to the top of Nelson's monument and, on my last visit, went to the cinema. The film was called Darby O'Gill and the Little People, starring Albert Sharpe, Janet Munro, and Sean Connery, and although it was supposed to be a film for children, it had a lasting effect on me. I had already received some aggravation from the pretty landlord's daughter for not knowing about the 'black and tans', or other parts of Irish history. To be truthful, I hadn't got much knowledge of any country's history, not even my own. But this was different. Nobody had warned me about the 'little people' who were living in the countryside and certainly not about the banshee, whose wailing is supposed to foretell the approaching death of a member of the family.

It had taken a Disney film to inform me.

Here I was, back in a strange dark room, lying in bed on my own (the lads had returned to

Belfast). I had 'downed' a few pints, and was thinking about where my ancestors had originated from, when thoughts of those little people kept coming into my mind. I had a thing about dwarfs as one had once chased me as a child at a fair.

Banshees and little people stayed with me all that night and by morning I was already planning a hasty retreat home.

*****

There were six consultant psychiatrists at the hospital, each having their own field of interest. One was the medical superintendent, three kept up to date with new forms of treatment, whilst the other two just plodded on. The admission wards were divided between them and they took responsibility for those patients brought into them. The patients on the long-stay wards were also allocated to them, but were not visited on a regular basis, partly because the consultant psychiatrists were responsible for over three hundred patients each and they had to concentrate on the acute side of their work. They relied heavily upon the nursing staff to keep them informed of problems and often took their advice on how to treat patients. The consultant psychiatrists were known to the staff as the RMO

(responsible medical officer) and each patient was allocated an RMO.

Charlie's ward, being an admission ward had two consultants allocated to it and they took responsibility for whatever patients were admitted on the day they were on call. (The only exception to this rule was that a psychiatrist would take a patient if they were readmitted and had previously been one of their cases.) Each psychiatrist had working with them a team of doctors and a psychiatric social worker.

Dr Minor visited the ward twice a week and he was on call the night that Charlie was admitted.

The first time Charlie met Dr Minor was in the charge nurses office. Patients always went to see the doctor, rarely the other way round. The doctor, a middle-aged portly gentleman was dressed in a dark pin-striped suit and wore spectacles. He was sitting behind the office desk drinking tea from a china cup with a plate of his favourite biscuits by his side.

The nurse-in-charge, tall and also middle-aged, stood beside the doctor. He was wearing a clean white coat which he had put on for the occasion. Another nurse waited outside but within earshot of what was going on and was 'available' if required.

Charlie soon realised that he was not there to make any comments about himself. In any case, nothing he said would influence his treatment.

Here in body, but not in soul he thought as the pair discussed his case. Eventually the doctor looked up at him and spoke.

'How do you feel Charlie? You've been a naughty boy, you know.'

But before Charlie could respond, the nurse-in-charge said;

'He's settling down with the medication you have prescribed, doctor.'

Charlie knew he was on Stelazine and Artane, known to him as two blues and a white.

(Stelazine is a tranquilliser and Artane is given with it to combat any drug induced extra-pyramidal symptoms).

'Good,' the doctor said. 'And how are you sleeping?'

'He is restless during the night,' the nurse replied.

Only because of the noises the night staff make, Charlie wanted to reply.

'We will review his night sedation,' said the doctor.

'And your appetite?'

'He eats everything put in front of him,' the nurse responded.

Not everything, Charlie thought.

'Bowels?'

'He says he is constipated doctor. Shall we give him an enema?'

'Yes do that.'

Enema from these sadistic bastards, Charlie thought. How can you shit here anyway, when there are only five bogs available and they all have filthy seats. They've got barn doors and there's no privacy.

Charlie started to fidget and his face went white with anger.

'Perhaps we should consider E.C.T,' added the nurse, revelling in his self-imposed role as the consultant's adviser.

'I'm not having that,' Charlie suddenly heard himself saying as he rose from his chair. 'Nurse,' the charge nurse shouted as Charlie approached him.

The door shot open and before Charlie could continue his protests he was bundled away and back to his bed. Dr Minor took out his gold knibbed fountain pen and wrote in Charlie's notes:

Examined today. Remains unpredictable and aggressive.

Advised nursing staff to keep him in the ward. To commence E.C.T.

Constipated: give soap and water enema, and Epsom salts.

Will review night sedation on next visit.

That was Charlie's first acquaintance with his responsible medical officer.

The nurses had been taught that an enema was an injection of water into the lower bowel. An evacuant enema is given for the purpose of emptying the lower bowel. Plain water is the simplest form and this is sometimes described as a simple enema, 'enema simplex', though the term was also generally used to describe a soap and water enema, more correctly designated 'enema saponis'.

An enema was a simple and routine procedure on Charlie's and other wards and a common procedure, especially for epileptic patients. Constipation often causes these patients to have fits. It was a simple procedure, Charlie was told, but unfortunately nothing was ever simple here. He was back in his bed for the rest of that day and his meals were brought to him on a tray.

'You are to have an enema,' the nurse told him, putting the screens around his bed. 'Get off your bed while I cover it with this rubber sheet.'

'Take your pyjama trousers off, then lie back on the bed, on your left side, then bring your knees up to your chest and relax,' he continued without drawing breath.

Charlie got off the bed, took off his pyjama bottoms, and was back lying down in the required position.

'So far, so good,' Charlie thought. Then 'Bog' appeared.

Bog was known to his nursing colleagues as the 'shit' nurse. He couldn't get enough of it and always volunteered to do the manual evacuations and enemas. He was a tubby, red-faced Welshman, and an ex-farm hand who thought that this background made him a good nurse. Down the dormitory he sailed, apron on, gloved hands up in the air, with his index finger on his right hand pointing to the sky, suitably greased ready to stick up Charlie's backside.

'Relax,' he said, but Charlie was off that bed like a shot, only to be restrained and put back in the required position.

The 'finger' and then practically the whole of Bog's hand were shoved up Charlie's backside. Charlie screamed, then cried, not only from the pain but also from the indignity that he was being forced to endure. When the hand was removed, a long rubber tube was inserted, two inches Charlie was told, it felt like two feet. Soapy water was poured into the funnel, down the tube and inside him.

'Hold it in you for as long as you can,' he was told. Charlie couldn't. It seemed to run straight out of him and so he was finally allowed to sit on a commode, his bowels opened, his eyes watered, and his spirit and dignity broken a

little bit more. To Charlie it was another lesson
in the learning process of survival. He never
complained of constipation again. To Bog?
well he recorded it as a good result.

*****

Having returned from my holiday early I had
time to spare before going back to work and so
I decided to ask for permission to move into
the nurses' home. Following my little
adventure in Ireland I now felt the need to
become more independent. It would also save
me from cycling back and forth to work each
day, a journey that was becoming tedious. I
approached the chief male nurse whose
permission was required to make the move. I
had to convince him that my need was
genuine, as the home was for staff who lived
away from the area. I told him I had domestic
problems and he finally agreed.
The senior nurses felt that the domestic affairs
of their staff was their business and some of
the younger nurses, if they wanted to get
married, had to seek approval from the matron
or chief male nurse. I was allocated a room on

the third floor, at the front of the home, just over the main entrance. It was small and basic, but suited my needs with a bed, small bedside locker, wardrobe and sink. The staff home provided accommodation for all grades of staff, including porters and ancillary staff, but most were nurses.

Home wardens were on duty twenty-four hours a day and staff like myself, under the age of eighteen, had to apply for late passes from the nursing office if they wanted to stay out after 10pm. There were four floors, and each had their own bathroom, toilet and kitchen facilities. All members of staff had their own rooms, and there was a television room situated on the top and bottom floors. A central recreation room was situated near the reception area where most of the staff congregated, and met each other.

I settled down into my new surroundings and on returning to work, found that a sister had been appointed to be responsible for the training and allocation of cadets. She reported to the matron and chief male nurse and assisted in the recruitment of new staff from the local schools. She turned out to be a pleasant person who met us all individually, telling us that she was there to train, support and advise us as we prepared to become nurses.

My next allocation was the Gymnasium. All the male cadets loved this placement, as they thought that they would be playing more than working. However, this was not always the case. I arrived just in time to assist with the preparation for the annual sports day and was kept extremely busy.
The Liverpool Regional Hospital Sports were held annually, during the summer months. They included most track and field events and were very competitive, especially between the three main mental hospitals in the region, The Deva, Rainhill and Winwick.
The first regional athletics meeting had taken place in 1956 under the presidency of T.Keeling Esq, CBE, JP, MA, Chairman of the Liverpool Regional Board. These were organised by the Deva Hospital group secretary and the venue was normally at one of the three large mental hospitals.
This year they were held at the Deva and I was

entered for most of the track events. This was because once all the nominations had been received for each event, the cadet nurses were called on, whether they wanted to or not, to fill in any gaps in the team. The first six places in each event scored points.

Each participating hospital brought a coach-load of supporters including staff and patients, whist the management committees put pressure on each team to win a trophy. There were three major trophies, the ladies' and the men's cup and the overall winner's trophy. The 'boss' the PTI, felt that failure was a slant on his ability to do his job and so pushed all the staff to train hard. Being allocated to the gym enabled me to train every day, as I particularly wanted to do well on my first appearance. I was a good runner for my age, but knew I was handicapped in having to compete against men. I was told that I would be expected to do well in the 880 yards, an event that I had competed for at Chester Schoolboy level.

The hospital provided all the kit, including the plimsolls and we spent hours cleaning them during our P.T. breaks. I was encouraged to run around the track, against my colleagues. It was smaller than the standard size and meant the half-mile was more than the normal two laps. The training methods were not very orthodox. In fact, the P.T. Instructor promised me a packet of five Woodbines for every occasion I could beat my previous best time. This did spur me on as I had been encouraged to smoke by the other cadets and was usually gasping for a fag. The cadets were reminded that the Deva team had won the trophy in 1956 and, as there were some good athletes on our hospital staff, were expected to do well again this year. The main rivalry was in the last event to take place, the men's tug of war.

The Deva team trained for months in advance, using a large tree at the bottom of the sport's field. A rope was threaded through a pulley which was tied to a bough of a tree. Heavy weights were attached to one end of the rope as the team member's attempted to pull it up, individually and together.

It all became very 'macho' with the older members trying to keep their place in the team, pressured by the bigger and stronger members of staff who were keen to take part. The team was enthusiastically trained by the 'boss' who shouted and bawled encouragement. The team members all wore heavy boots, and were taught how to 'dig in' and take the strain. When they did, you could hear the rope creak. Then they pulled the rope, heaving up the weights, which they held for as long as they could. This was usually until the weakest fell away, then they would all fall backwards, and lie on the ground puffing and cursing. Apart from the training, there was also a lot of work for the hospital hosting the sports. There was the track to mark out, tents to erect for changing rooms, catering and hospitality, and bunting was added to brighten up the field. Benches and chairs had to be brought from various parts of the hospital grounds and a P.A. system hired. On the day the cadets came in on their day off to help with the preparations and everyone soon got excited. The heats began for the sprint events and though I had already run twice before the half-mile took place, I still managed to finish a creditable third. However I still had to run in the men's relay, the last track event on the programme.

One of our Consultant's, Dr Middlefell, easily won the hammer and my best mate, Geoff, won a medal in the javelin. For the last event the Deva team had to win the tug-of-war, to give us enough points to take the overall trophy, and the men's cup. The final was against Rainhill hospital, and with much encouragement and shouting from the crowd, The Deva inched their way to victory, winning the best of three pulls.

A crate of beer was always available to the finalists and eagerly drunk by all the team members, except one. That was Tom, our deputy chief male nurse, who was a strict Methodist lay preacher. I thought he must have had 'strong religion' to refuse a drink on a red-hot summer's day when he was obviously parched.

Tom was a good nurse and well educated. He was known for always answering difficult questions with a parable, which was clever really. He usually got everyone so confused, they forgot what they had originally asked him.

There was a great sense of togetherness as all the staff celebrated, with the first three in each event receiving a medal. Everyone tucked into refreshments. Those who had been sent off

duty to represent the hospital took a shower.
Tug-of -war was also popular at the annual
patients' fete, an event that included games,
competitions, and entertainment. The fete was
held on the field in front of the hospital and
was attended by staff, patients and people from
the local community. Many of the locals
supported hospital functions and some
belonged to the patients' league of friends, to
provide extra comforts and visits.

Streamers and buntings were draped around
the front of the hospital and a small fair came
with roundabouts, swings, and stalls. There
was also Punch and Judy and rides in a horse
and cart around the grounds for the children of
staff.

The hospital had its own games and stalls that
were stored and brought out year after year.
There was a beam for a pillow fight, hoopla
and a favourite called 'Tilt the bucket', which
was designed to soak a volunteer with water.
This always drew a crowd when a senior
member of staff sat below the bucket and it
certainly boosted funds as everyone wanted to
be the first to soak them.

I thought it a memorable sight when a near-empty field suddenly filled up with spectators as each ward brought out most of their occupants dressed up in their Sunday best. As I had observed at the film show, it was noticeable how the men sat on one side of the field and the women on the other. This was the rigid segregation of the male and female patients, though I had been told that the practice was about to be broken.

Many of the patients were allowed to walk of their own volition around the stalls, which meant they headed in the same direction towards the refreshment tent. For security reasons, staff took it in turns to patrol the hospital entrance to ensure that nobody wandered off. The nurses took along extra sweets and cigarettes and patients would eagerly await their turn for these extra treats.

The fete literally buzzed with its own special atmosphere and many patients had been looking forward to the day for weeks. Following a musical fanfare, a local dignity opened the fete and then there was followed a display of gymnastics by a combined team of staff and patients who were all dressed in white trousers and vest; I had spent days making sure all the pumps were spotlessly white. Later a fancy dress parade was staged and various games took place for the patients to compete in, such as the egg and spoon and sack race, and for those who were able, running and field events. Then, of course, before the patients returned to their wards, there was the jelly and blancmange, sandwiches and cakes.

*****

Days turned into weeks and although Charlie was on an admission ward there seemed little to occupy the patients who had been there for a while. The staff were kept busy looking after the more acute, or disturbed patients, and so most of the others just sat around doing nothing. This led to apathy and melancholy, so the slow, but inevitable institutionalisation of many of the patients started quite soon after their admissions.

A few went home, cured, but others often returned within several months as there was

little stimulation in the environment they had
been discharged to. The remainder were
transferred to long-stay wards and the odd one,
like Charlie, stayed and were allocated work.
It was usually the long-stay patients who did
the manual work, such as delivering coal to the
wards, working on the farms, or being part of
the barrow gangs engaged in keeping the
grounds tidy.
Charlie would watch the barrow gang pass his
ward. He counted over seventy men one day,
all trooping past in a world of their own. Some
had their heads down, others grinned and
talked to themselves, and some wandered
away from the organised line of insanity, only
to be shunted back to their places by attendants
and nurses. They all wore boots, overcoats,
and caps, which made them all look the
same...the uniform of insanity, Charlie
thought.
He began to look out for different ones as they
passed. They had their own mannerisms, and
his favourite one was the man who did a twirl
every now and again. Whatever the weather he
always seemed happy.
Charlie's first jobs, as he was not allowed

unescorted out of the ward, was to clean all the
brass and also assist in the kitchen. Each week,
a rota was displayed on a notice board for
those patients capable of helping with the
washing and drying of the dishes and utensils
after each meal. The cleaning of the brasses
turned out to be a bigger task than Charlie had
anticipated. It included all the doorknobs, and
locks in the ward, the brass part of the fire
hyphen, and the cutlery once a week. The ward
cutlery consisted of over fifty knives, forks,
and spoons. For this task he was supervised by
one of the staff and helped by other patients.
Most of this cutlery was kept in a locked knife
box. Every night the staff were not allowed off
duty until every item was accounted for and
the daily ward report required the nurse-in-
charge to state that all cutlery was correct.
Charlie's first taste of adventure came
unexpectedly. It was about four o'clock on a
pleasant summer's day. Charlie was cleaning
the ward door knobs when a young cadet nurse
let himself into the ward.
'Let me clean the outside knobs,' Charlie said
jokingly, and to his surprise he did. Not only
did he let him out, he locked him out.

Charlie's emotions were mixed, mildly exhilarated, but afraid. At first he just stood there. He was confused about what to do, but then instinct took over, and he walked down the corridor and out into the garden. Although his senses were numbed by his medication, he felt amazed that he had forgotten how it felt to feel the sun shining and hear the birds singing. There were people sitting on seats in the corner, but they never even looked at him, let alone challenged him.

Perhaps I look normal, carrying these tins and rags he said to himself. They perhaps think I'm a workman. Then panic overcame him and he ran back to the ward, arriving just as the cadet was leaving.

'Let me in,' said Charlie...and no one was any wiser.

The experience left him shaking and later he was full of regrets as to what could have happened. Escape, escape from this nightmare and never return. He couldn't eat his supper and that night, lying in bed, his emotions were mixed.

Why didn't I run away when I had the chance? he mused.

Did he want to run away, or was he getting too dependent on this place?

The warmth of the sun on his face and the few minutes he had spent without being observed had stirred up something inside him. He must get out.

He consoled himself that this was another learning experience and he was right not to have tried to leave; he would not have lasted long and had nowhere to go. He also reminded himself that any attempt to get away would have alerted staff of his intention to abscond and any future attempts would be impossible. He would also have lost the few hard   earned privileges he had.

Charlie drifted off to his first trouble free sleep for ages...not to the sound of the birds, but to the sound of snoring and the passing of wind. Yet those sounds were somehow sweeter tonight.

Entrance to the main buildings.

Chapter four.

I was football daft and always wanted to play
centre forward, but was never good enough
and so, at school, I ended up on the right wing,
using my ability to sprint to compensate for
my shortfalls in football skills. I was therefore
excited when the chance did come to play 'up
front', even though it was only for the hospital
patients' team.
Like the staff team, the patients also competed
against each other. Sometimes they would
travel to a game as far away as the Midlands.
This would take up a whole day and was
popular with those who liked to get out and
about. Patients teams could include staff and
this was by mutual agreement with the other
side, three normally being the maximum
number acceptable. This was justified with the
excuse that it added interest to the fixture and
provided encouragement and support for the
patients, as occasionally a few did lose the
plot.
Some of the patients were very good
footballers, but there was never quite enough
of them to make a winning team, even though

it did include staff. One or two reluctant
patient 'volunteers' needed a gentle reminder to
participate in the game or they would just
stand around and lose interest.

My debut was against a Warrington hospital
and our team included a Portuguese nurse,
who was said to be tricky, and the 'boss', the
PTI, who played every game as if was the cup
final. He would bellow and shout at everyone,
and dispute every decision.

Unfortunately, on this occasion the referee was
a patient from the visiting team and was
difficult to influence, especially as his own
staff were briefing him.

From the kick off I passed the ball to the
patient next to me and he promptly kicked it to
an opposing forward who raced for goal only
to be upended by the 'boss'.

'Penalty' shouted the ref who nearly tripped
himself up as he ran around in his long baggy
shorts.

'Blow your whistle,' somebody shouted, which
he did, minutes after the incident, and straight
down the 'boss's' ear.

'Nonsense,' shouted the 'boss', confronting the
official. 'You must be mad awarding a penalty

for that.'
'He is,' said the opponent who had been fouled, picking up the ball and scoring from the penalty spot.

I decided to bring the Portuguese nurse, our star player, from the wing so that he would receive the ball from the kick off. He looked impressive, wearing his own tight shorts, especially standing next to me, as mine were far too long. As soon as he got the ball he beat everybody in sight, a real Stanley Mathews, 'the wizard of dribble'. As he went passed one mesmerised opponent after another, mostly patients, he acknowledged his artistry with a shout of delight. The only problem was that he would not pass to anybody else and eventually ran out of steam when the ball crossed the line and out of play.

At half time it was 1-0 to the opposition as the 'boss', once he had got over his his anger from the penalty decision, had been dominant in defence and 'slowed' down their goal scorer. I was hoping not to have to play in the second half because the match was turning into a farce.

The referee, having been encouraged to blow

his whistle, had done so with gusto and was being mostly ignored as the staff were actually controlling the match by mutual consent. I was reminded that I was there for the benefit of the patients and so reluctantly took the field for the second half. Meanwhile, a 'ringer' was introduced to our side, (a staff member, pretending to be a patient). This tactic turned the game around and although the opposition were suspicious, nothing was said, but the mood of the game changed.

The 'boss' was now back at Wembley and the team responded to his enthusiasm. To my delight, I scored a hat trick.

The first was scored after I tracked the 'star' and nipped in just when he was about to shoot. The 'star' chased me shouting obscenities, but I never heard him as I acknowledged the acclaim of the crowd, several watching patients. For the second I hit the ball through the goalie's legs whilst he was having his own private conversation with no-one in particular. The third, and I thought my best, was a glancing header, after the 'star' had finally decided to cross the ball. He had obviously forgiven me from the way he kissed me after that effort.

Each hospital provided excellent hospitality for their visitors who always received a hot meal in the winter, or a ham salad during the summer when they then played cricket. Everyone sat together and I found this an excellent opportunity to meet and exchange ideas with staff and patients from different backgrounds.

*****

Some of the many anxieties I had as a cadet nurse were about the treatments administered to patients. My thoughts, about the operating theatre, the insulin therapy unit and the refractory ward, were mainly formulated from stories and incidents related by colleagues. There was the one of sawing off a patient's leg and the nurse taking it away to the incinerator; there were others about holes being bored into people's heads and patients being put to sleep for days on end. Then there was a patient who could kick down the pads door and I certainly hoped I would never have to deal with him. By far the worst, and though I knew that all the tales were exaggerated, concerned giving patients electric shock treatments, E.C.T. (Electro-convulsive Therapy). This worried me the most because, when the time came to go on the wards, I wasn't sure I would be able to assist with E.C.T.

The sister in charge of cadets did much to allay our fears, telling us not to listen to what she called 'old wives tales'. During one of our training sessions she gave us a lecture on E.C.T., commencing with an outline of its history.

Convulsive therapy was introduced in 1934 by a Budapest-based psychiatrist, Ladisla von Meduna, who proposed ameliorating the symptoms of schizophrenia by deliberately putting patients into a convulsive state. He had become aware of changes seen in the brain of schizophrenics at autopsy, which he believed was different from patients suffering from epilepsy. In fact, he believed that some epileptics who developed schizophrenia suffered less fits. His experimental methods of inducing fits was by an injection of Cardiazol. Although first given for schizophrenia, it was soon found to be more effective for the treatment of depressive states. This original method of inducing fits by an injection of Cardiazol has a history of being unreliable and feared by many patients. It was replaced by the method of electrical induction in 1938. This was introduced by a professor of psychiatry in Rome, Ugo Cerletti, and one of his assistants, Lucio Bini. They had first tested this treatment on animals.

E.C.T had become a common and effective treatment for severe depression in the hospital, but Charlie for one was far from convinced. A junior doctor had described a case to him where an elderly lady had been close to death, through her inability to eat and drink, due to her poor mental state. He said that after several treatments with E.C.T. Her improvement was remarkable, and that E.C.T. probably saved her life. This had impressed the listening staff, but not Charlie who was still dubious about its use, especially on him.

E.C.T. was explained to Charlie as being a safe and effective treatment that would help to hasten his recovery. He was told that he would be put to sleep, a phrase that did not instil a lot of confidence in him, as several dogs in his household had been led away for a similar experience, and had naturally failed to return. Charlie was also told that whilst asleep, an electrical current would be administered to his head, inducing a fit, and after a short sleep he would wake up and, apart from perhaps a headache and loss of memory he would be fine. The loss of memory would only be temporary and there was no danger of important things being forgotten.

After several treatments, Charlie was assured, he should begin to feel better. However, he felt sick and his body trembled. The words 'electro,' and 'convulsive,' had unnerved him and left a hollow empty feeling in his stomach. The very thought of an electric current being passed through his brain terrified him.

Worse, when he expressed his concerns, he was told he had no say in the matter as he was certified.

Charlie was supposed to have been introduced to a patient who had benefited from the treatment, but he never was. Instead, quite the opposite happened. He met a patient who had been having E.C.T. for years and Charlie thought he seemed 'scrambled'.

That night Charlie slept very little. The treatment was to start the following day and would continue twice a week for three to six weeks and then be reviewed.

On this ward the E.C.T. was carried out in the dormitory and patients were put in a row of beds next to each other. Charlie was number four.

Two trolleys were wheeled out of the clinic and into the dormitory. One had the medical and resuscitation equipment on it, including a row of drawn up syringes. The other had the 'box', as the staff called the E.C.T. machine. This was the apparatus for giving the treatment, and what the electrodes were plugged into. There was also a bowl of red solution, into which the electrodes were dipped, some rubber mouth gags and wooden back supports, which were padded.

Charlie's fear intensified when he saw the nurse examining the electrodes, shaking the excessive fluid from them. The doctor arrived and a screen was placed between the first and second beds. More nurses arrived and the treatment began. Charlie, who had a parched mouth from an Atropine injection, soon realised it was possible to see through the screens at what was going on, with the patients ahead of him, though he refrained from doing so...the sounds were bad enough.

'Have you got your false teeth in?'

'Right, hold his arm out, while I put him to sleep.'

'I can't find a vein, put the tourniquet on his arm, nurse.'

Charlie was following the sequence of the treatment down to the intravenous injection of Pentothal and Scoline, an anaesthetic and muscle relaxant.

'Ow! you're hurting me,' he heard the patient say.

'Be quiet you noisy bugger, help me hold him down.'

In goes the mouth gag.

'Right that's it, Are you ready? Hold on to his limbs.'

The shock treatment was administered.

'That's a good fit, ready, turn him on his side.'

Lots of gurgling, then snoring, sucking out and resuscitation.

Noise of screens being moved, idle chatter, getting nearer.

Now its Charlie's turn and the screens are moved around his bed. Then they encircle him...white coats and eyes and arms seem everywhere.

Events take over. Charlie has no time to think, but give them their due they are efficient and quick.

'I need a pee,' said Charlie.

'Why didn't you ask before? There's no time now.'

'Ready doctor, hold out your arm...'

Later, much later, Charlie awoke with what seemed like a terrible hangover.

'Where am I? Christ, I feel terrible,' he moaned.

'When am I having my treatment?'

And so it went on for the next six weeks. Altogether Charlie had twelve treatments. He was allowed up after the first and was soon back to his daily routine, which still included cleaning the brass on the ward, and although he was unaware of it, due to his lack of insight into his illness, E.C.T. was improving his general state of health.

It was pointed out to him by the staff that he was paying more attention to his personal appearance and was becoming more involved with ward activities. Charlie had not really noticed. He had other things on his mind, like getting out.

One night, Len, a large, heavy set man of about forty-five, was admitted to the ward and, after the enforced period in his pyjamas, was moved to the bed next to Charlie. He was a man of few words which suited Charlie as he had had his fair share of noisy, and disruptive patients sleeping next to him. Len was the kind of guy who demanded respect, even though he spoke very little. Even the staff were more forthcoming to his needs. He started E.C.T. about the same time as Charlie, and it was noticed by other patients that he was always done first or second.

Charlie had asked to be considered for that privileged spot. First in the queue, so to speak, get it over and done with and avoid the awful wait. It occurred to Charlie that the most dangerous or difficult you were, the quicker you were done, i.e. unless it was a patient who was 'boxed' up and left until last because the heavy gang was normally required.

Charlie had been told that some of the patients,

if they couldn't be handled or held down long enough to be given the needle, were given E.C.T. 'straight' without an anaesthetic.

The first indication to Charlie that things were amiss was when he woke up in the early hours and thought he heard Len crying from pain. The next day he noticed the look in Len's eyes had changed from menacing to deep and more thoughtful. Patients were good at interpreting looks and moods in each other as their own welfare often depended upon it. The next thing Charlie noticed was that Len became more intense at night time, often lying on his bed staring at the ceiling, but not staring aimlessly, more like thinking and planning something. Charlie knew that they all sat around for much of the day thinking, or day-dreaming, some of them even had voices to listen to, but Len, he was different. He was definitely planning something.

Charlie knew very little about him. He always looked clean and tidy, kept himself to himself and appeared to know the ropes, which meant he had probably been in here before. He was responsive to senior staff, but Charlie somehow felt he dismissed them in his mind.

He appeared to be intelligent, but never seemed to read or listen to the wireless. Unlike Charlie, he seemed unconcerned about the E.C.T...with a do it if you must attitude, and then leave me alone.

The doctor, when he came, always saw Len at his bedside, so perhaps he was important or wealthy, but if he was, he never had any visitors. Charlie just couldn't fathom him, but he was sure he was up to no good.

It happened when Charlie least expected it and the staff had reacted like lightening. Early one morning, when the staff were changing shifts. Len had shot up in bed, screaming 'shite' at the top of his voice.

'Shite,' he shouted again, obviously in pain, diving out of his bed and running around the dormitory.

'Crap,' Charlie shouted taking evasive action by hiding underneath his bed.

'Shit,' shouted a nurse as he rushed towards Len who was heading towards the door with faecal matter pouring everywhere. A bigger pantomime you would never see again. Staff were appearing from everywhere. There was shite in Len's bed, on the floor, up the walls, and before they caught him, on the staff.

Len was put into a bath, and afterwards, Charlie thought he had a kind of peaceful look on his face. No wonder, he thought, getting all that off his mind. When he was ordered to help clean up the mess, he also thought he caught a mocking look in Len's eyes.

There was not many patients who could say that they had shit on the staff!

Charlie later learned that Len, amongst other things, suffered from chronic constipation and was always moody and unpredictable until his bowels opened. He must have been very uncomfortable and the night nurse, having experienced this behaviour before, had given him a large dose of Epsom salts...but was hoping to get off duty before the inevitable explosion.

Charlie knew from his own experience that they attributed constipation with the cause of an exacerbation of patient's symptoms and many of the epileptics had fits due to it, hence the reason for the bowel book which was religiously filled in each day.

Charlie wondered why 'Bog' never visited Len to give him one of his notorious enemas.

Chapter five.

I had settled down at the hospital, too settled
really, as sometimes I never left the hospital
grounds for days on end. The worse time was
weekends and public holidays, as my friends
would go home and it was boring to sit in a
small room without any money and nothing
much to do. I did run up the canal bank daily,
training for my next race, but there was no
need to really as the daily PT sessions kept me
fit. At night I would sit in the recreation hall as
I was interested in courting one of the female
cadets and sometimes she would be there.
There were more female cadets than males,
and we were sometimes employed in the same
department, such as the pharmacy.
Just as the lad's placements included the
Barber's shop and Tailor's, the girls went to the
Ladies Hairdresser's and the Sewing room.
The discipline for the female cadets was very
strict if they lived in. The hospital took its
responsibility very seriously and each night
cadets had to account for themselves to the
home wardens, two-middle aged ladies who
were strict, but fair. They were also very

supportive and I regarded one of them as a 'favourite aunt.' She would sit with us in the recreational room and have a good old natter. An essential part of the cadet nursing scheme was education. It was twofold. One aspect was to prepare cadets for future nurse training and the other was was to assess their suitability to undergo this training. The personality of the cadet was important, as they would have to nurse many difficult people. Because they only had a three-year contract they were not guaranteed a place in the school of nursing, but it was fair to say that none of us felt any pressure as we expected to be successful. The drop out rate for cadets was low.

All the cadets attended the local college of further education, twice a week, and we really stood out and felt awkward as we still had to wear our uniforms. We studied Maths, English, Human Biology and Hygiene, for our G.C.E. Examinations. We also had a choice of doing Woodwork, Art, History, and Cookery.

I chose to study history as I was particularly interested in the local history of Chester and had been a regular visitor to the museum since I was a child. Deva was the Roman name for

Chester, hence the name of the hospital. There were other examples locally such as the Deva Hotel and Deva Lane which was situated in the hospital grounds where some of the staff houses were.

I also thought it would be a good idea to extend my knowledge of the health service by studying the history of mental illness and the Deva's relationship with the local community. At first, my college tutor was surprised at my choice of subject. He was used to teaching the broader sense of history, but as this lesson was more of a fill in, he smiled and suggested we might both learn something. In fact, by the next lesson, he had done some homework himself and told me how to get started. He had read that the study of mental illness was comparatively new, even though the existence of abnormal behaviour had been recognised since the beginning of time. Some of the people in the old testament of the bible had suffered mood swings, depression and delusions. To a degree, the classic writings of the Greeks and Romans understood and taught the importance of the mind. He said that it had really got him thinking in a different way, as to

how some of the characters of the past had
behaved.

I learned that the fate of the mentally ill was
both tragic and horrific in the Middle ages,
when they were tortured and even put to death,
as they were regarded as being possessed by
the devil, or an evil spirit. One way or the
other, the mentally ill were always treated
badly, being ridiculed or ill-treated. I was
horrified by some of the things that I read, and
soon realised that those who condemned and
persecuted them were themselves mentally ill,
often paranoid or psychotic.

It was not until the early years of the
nineteenth century that some members of
society began to show concern for the welfare
of the insane, although I am sure there were
compassionate people throughout the ages
who didn't get recognition for their good
deeds.

The first person to be given credit for his role
as an advocate and champion for the mentally
insane was a Frenchman, Philippe Pinel, who
removed the chains from patients at the
Bicetre Hospital in Paris. When you consider
public-thinking of the day, he must have been

a very brave and enlightened man.

In England, William Tuke, who opened the York retreat in 1796, replaced punishment and solitary confinement by humanitarian methods, including occupation of all kinds. I learned that the Deva hospital had opened as an asylum in 1829 and has subsequently been known by various names. When the National health service was created it became 'Upton Mental Hospital', Upton being the area in which the hospital was situated. Early in the 1950s, it became the Deva Hospital.

Records show that the hospital was originally built on a ten-acre site and consisted of a central administration block of four storeys, with two wings, one on each side, and three storeys in height. The hospital at the time was built to cater for the needs of ninety patients, equal men and women living in separate wings. Twenty of these patients paid for their own rooms, whilst the remainder were classed as pauper patients, and their respective parishes and towns financed their keep. The staff consisted of one resident matron, twelve attendants and two part-time doctors.

A Dr Thomas Nadauld Brushfield, regarded as

a specialist in mental illness was appointed as
the first resident Medical Superintendent and
was in the post from 1854-1865. Dr Brushfield
was also a member of the local Archaeology
and Historic Society, and became notable for
his knowledge and written articles and books.
During the first half of the 1800s, conditions at
the Chester, and other similar establishments
were poor. The accommodation consisted of
straw beds and pillows and patients were
forced to eat on the floor, from rubber and
metal bowls using wooden spoons.
There was also a strong emphasis on restraint,
and metal rings attached to the walls, were
used to secure patients in metal waist and
wristbands. A senior nurse who had studied the
old records told me there were no night staff
and there was only a ratio of one nurse to
twenty five patients.
I learned that the infamous Lillie Langtry's
husband had died at the hospital in October
1897. Edward Langtry had left his wife years
before his admission. Having been found in a
confused state near Crewe railway station he
had been brought to the asylum by the police,
suffering from the effects of a serious head

injury. He died just over a week later and is buried in the Overleigh Cemetery, Handbridge, Chester, near to where my own family graves are sited.

Langtry's death reminded me that I had a copy of a report of the committee of Visitors of the Cheshire County Asylum dated April 1854. It started by stating that, the deaths during the previous year had decreased.

For 1852..............32 out of a daily average of 236.

For 1853..............28 out of a daily average of 243.

I could not make up my mind if these figures were a criticism, or meant as praise-it seemed strange to start a report with the annual death rate.

Most of the male wards had snooker tables in the day room.

*****

The days and weeks moved on, although the days seemed endless to Charlie. He was becoming too settled in the ward. He had seen the Consultant psychiatrist, Dr Minor again, and because he had learned to keep quiet, and be respectful, when it mattered, had received a favourable report. He was given ground parole, which would enable him to attend some of the hospital functions.

The ward environment remained tranquil most of the time, although the odd outburst of violent behaviour, and petty squabbles persisted. This was only to be expected when the boredom of enforced confinement frayed the nerves, as most patients became fed up with the regular and unchanging routines of the ward.

The unchecked behaviour of some of the new admissions did relieve the boredom sometimes, even if it was unwelcome behaviour at times.

Charlie thought back to the time of his own admission, what bit he remembered of it.

Did I act like that? He asked himself when he saw a patient chance his luck, by questioning his treatment, or disobeying the ward orders. He could now see how chaotic things could become without this discipline and routine. How dull I must be becoming, he thought.

Not all the patients' behaviour was dangerous, or threatening. Some were quite docile, and Charlie wondered why they were here. Some patients behaviour could be hilarious, especially those who were manic. Not that Charlie would mock, but he could not not help laughing at times, as the staff did. Not laughing at the patient, but laughing with them. The manic patient at the height of his illness could wreck the ward routine and test the patience of Job.

Some would rush around leaving on taps, piling up chairs, and turning on the lights. They would be physically and mentally alert, as they dashed around, and often never stopped talking. They would would answer everybody, whether they were talking to them or not, with witty comments, or nonsense, faster then a stand up comic.

Charlie and the other patients soon got up fed up with them and became annoyed when a patient in his manic state, interfered with their belongings and routine. Fights could break out when items were taken, which often made matters worse. Manic patients did not respond to reason, in fact their behaviour often became more disturbed, if they were challenged. Everybody would give a sigh of relief, when the charge nurse decided enough was enough and confined the patient to a side room. Not that it stopped there. The patient would bang on the door of his room or sing or shout, and pile up his bed and furniture against the wall or side room door. Often the furniture and bed would have to be removed, and the patient would end up being nursed on a mattress on the floor, for his own safety.

Each day of the week was known for the activities taking place in the hospital on that particular day. Monday was the patients dance. Tuesday was parcel day, providing extra comforts for those entitled to them, with such things as sweets and cigarettes. Thursday was pay day and also picture day.

Each ward had its own set of daily routines, such as bath day, the doctor's visiting day. There were days for trips out. Some were local, like visiting the swimming baths, or playing football, others were a visit to the pub. Each ward had an annual day trip, when they visited the seaside or another destination of their choice; even annual holidays were being considered.

Charlie liked parcel day, because as a worker he was entitled to cigarettes, enough to last the week if he was careful. Some of the patients who had no financial means, received these extra comforts, and patients who worked also

received 'incentive money' in cash or 'kind'.
Other patients with their own money were also
allocated this on a weekly basis, The parcels
were sent from the hospital shop in white
paper bags, and contained their sweets,
tobacco, cigarettes and toiletries. It was the
usual practice for some of the patients to have
their cigarettes saved, so they would be given
some each day, otherwise they would smoke
them and be without for the rest of the week.
Other patients received a twist of shag tobacco
from which they rolled their own cigarettes.
The smoke from these cigar-like delights hung
around for hours and when the tobacco ran
out, some just smoked rolled paper.
Charlie, now allowed out, usually visited the
patients' shop, which was situated in the main
building, opposite the staff restaurant. He was
now able to purchase sweets and tobacco
himself. Newspapers were also on sale, but he
usually read one of the free ones delivered to
the ward each day.
There were cafe facilities in the shop where he
could buy a cup of tea or coffee. Some of the
patients spent most of the day there, drinking
gallons of tea and smoking.

The staff, especially the workmen, ancillary
staff and cadet nurses, spent their breaks there
and a period was allocated for staff only to use
the facilities. The shop was becoming shabby
in appearance, yet welcoming and homely, and
for a time a jukebox was situated at the bottom
of the room. It was always smoke-filled and
the once-white ceiling had turned brown.
Charlie liked to sit and listen to the music
when it was on, which was not often as there
always seemed to be a continual battle
between the cadets and shop manageress as
they competed for how loud a record should be
played. He would sit there with a blank look
on his face-his best tactic was to remain
inconspicuous so he would be left alone-
otherwise, like the other customers, he would
be continually pestered by some of the patients
asking for a cigarette or money. Some would
stand over him waiting for him to throw his
stump away which, when discarded, they
would smoke until it burned their fingers.
Charlie would watch a cadet nurse come into
the canteen, buy a cup of coffee, select a
record and turn up the sound at the back of the
jukebox, usually when he thought nobody was

watching.

On this occasion, the record chosen was a favourite of Charlie's, 'Move It' by Cliff Richard, and the Shadows. This has a 'heavy' bass sound and appeared to be the part of the record that was either your favourite or it annoyed you, depending on your taste. Cliff would start, 'Come on everybody let's move it and...,' but before it got much further, the shop manageress, complaining loudly to anybody who would listen, would turn the volume down.

Before she was hardly back in the shop, up would get a cadet nurse to put on another record. Slim Whitman was often the next to be played, and up it would go. Then down came the manageress and down went the music. Up and down, up and down, and then the last straw, out came the plug and that was the end of the music for that part of the day. Charlie watched this daily 'pantomime' without comment, and often asked himself who was the daftest, him or them.

His attention would then switch to the occupants of the shop. There could be anything from five to fifty people, depending on which ward was visiting or whether it was visiting day. The main attraction was a patient called Eric who got on Charlie's nerves at times.

He was a small, thin chap, middle-aged and always wore a dirty cloth cap. The way he wore his glasses gave him the appearance of being educated, and in a way he was.

He was always either writing reams of rubbish in a notebook, or talking manically into his tobacco tin. He was never quiet and yet Charlie had noticed that he was capable of looking after himself and assisted the tinsmith, when he was in the right frame of mind.

Often he gave a running commentary on what was going on, speaking into the tin as if it was a microphone. He also used to flirt with the women which Charlie thought was remarkable, looking at the state of him.

As the shop manageress rushed down the canteen to turn down the music he would stop rolling his cigarettes that were spread all over the table, with bits of tobacco everywhere, and away he would go.

'There she goes, the daft bat,' he would say. 'Running down to turn the music off.'

'Why, hello there beautiful-how are you?' he
continued as his mind turned to a pretty girl
cadet coming into his view.
'You can't call that music, its the devil's music.'
'There she goes, clipperty clop, when she
comes back the music will stop.'
A quick look up to make sure he was the
centre of attention and then on he would go.
'It's that bloody fool Arthur on the ward today,
its stew for dinner so I can't stay,'
Then, 'Billy's going for a cup of tea, he pissed
his trousers for us all to see.'
And, 'she's nice, Hello darling, I'm free.'
So it went on, continual chatter, into the tin,
stopping only as he rolled another fag. Hour
after hour, day after day. Charlie had heard that
he even kept it up in bed, head under the
blankets, talking away.
'Shut up, Eric,' somebody would shout.
'I don't listen to fools,' would be the reply and
off he would go again, on another line of
thought.
'With a beak like that I could make you honk,'
he would sneer to the long-nosed, unfortunate
workman passing by.
On and on it went until Charlie, like the others,

would get up and leave, no longer amused, just annoyed and unable to take any more.

A thing Charlie had noticed was that Eric could taper down his behaviour when it suited him, especially when the chief male nurse appeared, or when he wanted to go out on a trip, though once on the bus, off he would go again. The more attention he received, the worse he got, especially from pretty girl cadets who adored him, but then they could escape from his ramblings, couldn't they?

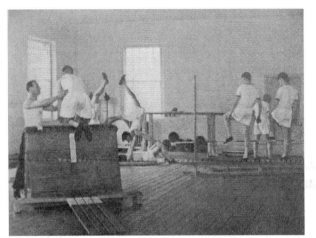

Male cadets were required to participate in physical activities twice a day.

Chapter six.

Many foreign staff were recruited to the hospital during the fifties and sixties as it was difficult to fill vacancies locally. Like most of my classmates I had a choice of employment when I left school. The recruitment of staff (especially for male nurses) was very competitive, with opportunities in the police, the armed forces, and the availability of apprenticeships being offered by local industry. The wages in nursing were very poor, the work was demanding and the position of a male nurse in a mental hospital was not really understood by the public...and not seen by most people, including my friends, as a position to be in.

I had continued to pursue my research into the history of the hospital and had been given some recent hospital reports which dealt with recruitment, and staffing problems.

I found out that in 1957 the hospital secretary, in his annual report, had stated 'that he would pursue the recruitment of foreign nurses to avoid the closure of wards.' It was the practice of that time, for the hospital secretary to advertise or even visit other countries on recruitment drives. The report stated that in 1956 that the hospital had twenty-nine foreign nurses and other staff.

Sixteen from Austria, 3 from Germany, 2 from Portugal, 2 from France,
2 Polish, I Spanish, 1 Belgian, 1 Cantonese and 1 West Indian. They all lived in hospital accommodation, and the report stated that a new home warden for the nurses home had been appointed, Mr E.P. Keevney, and this had considerably eased the problem of this 'polyglot staff'.

Some were employed as nurses, or orderlies, others as ancillary staff, working in the kitchens, laundry and stores. Many did not speak much English, which all added to the confusion of the place.

The number of staff from Portugal, Spain, and Africa increased at the hospital in the early sixties, and medical staff from Asia also began to arrive. These new recruits started at the end of the summer holidays, as that is when the recruitment drive usually happened, with the management mixing business with pleasure... Although they said it was no holiday, as recruiting staff from these countries was hard work.

A large number of staff came to work at the hospital from Ireland. Many came from Co. Armagh and this area seemed a good source of recruitment as a lot of the Irish men and women encouraged their friends to come over and start a career in nursing. The Irish lads also got involved with the social side of the hospital activities, especially with the entertainment held in the staff social club. Some of the staff recruited from other countries did have problems with adapting to working in the hospital, getting used to a new culture, and the environment of the mental hospital. I had problems myself, and I was a local lad, so it was really difficult for them. A few became home sick, others hadn't appreciated the nature of the work they were coming to, and some left for better paid jobs. But most to their credit stuck it out, and some ended up with senior positions on the staff. The main difficulties that were identified were mainly communication problems and cultural differences. Some of the staff employed at the hospital could not make themselves understood, mainly due to a lack of knowledge of the English language. I could never understand how these people were employed, because as a cadet nurse working in the manager's office I had been aware of them sending for staff to come and translate application forms. It therefore made it difficult, if not impossible for them to communicate with most of the patients, many of whom were already suffering from confusion.

Also, there was occasional problems in the way that some of the staff treated other staff and patients, due to their own ways at home. Some harshly treated members of the opposite sex as well as junior staff and their attitude towards the mentally ill created some problems on the ward. Likewise, some of the patients would not accept being nursed by 'foreigners,' as they called them, and some patients had been there so long they had never seen a 'foreigner' before.

Due to the multi-cultural nature of the staff and the different temperaments, there were inevitably quite a lot of differing opinions and petty squabbles which sometimes turned out to be full-scale fights occurred.

Although under age, I was still able to become a member of the staff social club, where I liked to call after work to meet my mates.

The club had been founded by the hospital staff and was run by them in their spare time. They had occupied several venues, which had been leased to them by management, and although the present building was limited in size, it had a good atmosphere, and was a popular place to meet. My friends and I would often stay there until closing time on payday, playing darts or the sixpenny fruit machine. Because of the limited space, I found that this made the place cosy, but it also could have a bad effect, because if anybody got noisy or boisterous, it could annoy the other members, hence the occasional fight.

Charlie liked nothing better than wandering around the grounds when he had time on his hands...and he had plenty of that. His movements away from the ward were restricted, so he was only allowed out for an hour or so in the afternoon, and this was recorded on his parole card, which he carried around in his pocket.

Each ward had its own airing court and
garden, secured by hedging and and railings,
and the steps to the upstairs wards were
covered with wire mesh, to prevent attempts of
self-harm.
Charlie spent a lot of time exploring the nooks
and crannies around the grounds. Some of the
patients had their own little hiding-places,
where they went to daily, and once discovered,
they could be found if necessary, as the staff
got to know where they were.
The hospital, in its spacious grounds was like a
small town, and self sufficient in providing for
a lot of its needs. With nearly 2000 patients
and all its different grades of staff, it was a
busy, and close knit community.
Charlie soon got to know other patients, and
many of the staff, who would greet him when
they saw him wandering around. Some of the
patients could be seen slowly walking around
with their heads down, arms by their sides, and
a vacant look on their face. They were really
institutionalised, and Charlie was told that they
were like that, because they were walking
around without a purpose in their life. They
had nowhere to go, with nothing to do, just

walking.

He promised himself that he would not end up like that, so made an effort to have a purpose to his walks.

He would visit the farm, to see the pigs and cattle, where he got to talk to the farm manager, who had noticed his interest in animals. He told Charlie that last years wet and sunless summer had not affected them obtaining a high yield of crops. He also warned Charlie not to hang around when nobody was around, as some of the tools and machinery were dangerous.

Charlie also tried to occupy himself by looking at the different buildings in the grounds noting their shapes and sizes. Once he had even tried to sharpen up his senses by counting the bricks in the chimney, but he never got very far up, as he couldn't concentrate for long enough, to get to the top, and it made him feel light headed. The chimney was massive, towering over all the other buildings, a landmark for miles around, together with the nearby water tower. Charlie also liked to lie in the grass, watching the smoke come out of the chimney, and disappear into the sky. Sometimes it was black and sometimes it was white, sometimes it went straight up, and other times it was blown quickly away by the wind. He was fascinated by smoke, it reminded him of the big open fire in his granny's house where, as a child, he had watched it drift up the chimney. He had tried to change the colours and the way it went, by poking the fire when no one was looking He remembered burning things, which changed its colour. He would even spit into it, to make it sizzle, hoping it wouldn't hang there on the coal, lingering, so that his granny would see it when she came into the room. Charlie loved his granny and a lump would come into his throat when he remembered her. He wouldn't be here today if she was still alive, he often thought. Then he wouldn't have had the traumas of his childhood either. Her death had probably been the start of his problems and he hadn't coped with it.

'The things that surface when you have time on your hands,' he thought. Best to keep them hidden, but could he? They were always asking questions here, delving deeper and deeper. Forcing himself to change his thoughts, he got up ready to continue his exploring. He would make up new games as he was determined to keep his mind active. Some days he would visit the workmen's yard where the painter's, fitters and joiners were. The works department did most of the building, repairs, and decorating, and some of the patients with the necessary skills assisted them. Patients also assisted other tradesmen, such as the plumbers, tinsmith and upholsterer. Other days Charlie would visit the gardens with their large greenhouses and flowerbeds. This department maintained the grounds, sports fields, and bowling greens, which were situated in some of the male wards gardens. The gardeners provided flowers for the wards and church services, and displays for various dances and functions. They were experts in their field, annually entering flower shows, such as at the Southport show, and they won many top awards.

Out of bounds to Charlie, as he only had ground parole, were the two housing estates which provided accommodation for some of the staff and their families. Other staff could live in, either in the large staff home or the flats at the front of the hospital.

The chief male nurse lived in the house by the entrance, and regularly stopped patients who had wandered by.

Charlie had heard that he also stood at the window, and 'clocked' staff that were late and those who went home early.

One day Charlie decided to chance his luck and walk to the nearby canal, which was situated at the back of the hospital. He walked along the path that led through the farm, then down on to the track that led across a field, over the stile and on to the canal, which had a quaint little bridge crossing it. From the top of the bridge he could see the gangs of patients working in the fields in the area known as the Willows, named after some of the trees growing there. Some patients were digging in the fields, while others were cutting wood. A fire nearby sent a swirl of smoke dancing towards the clouds. Charlie felt at peace here, so he sat against the wall of the bridge, and lit a cigarette; he blew the smoke out, trying to match the pattern of the smoke from the distant fire.

Lapwings called from the fields nearby, while a moor-hen darted in and out of the reeds.

Peace, perfect peace thought Charlie, relishing in his new-found freedom.

He could never have imagined himself sitting here six months ago, how quickly the time had gone since his admission. There had been talk of a transfer to a long-stay ward, which could happen any day now. He had only managed to stay where he was by working hard on the ward, and being pleasant to all around him. Being street wise, from a young age, he had quickly learned that the bad patients were got rid of quickly, while the good ones were held on to by the charge nurse as long as was possible.

'Pass on the problems to another ward,' he had heard him say. But the senior staff were now questioning how long he had been on the admission ward, so his move would come.

He lit another cigarette. This time he held it in front of his face and let the smoke rise in front of him. He would gently blow, watching the patterns of smoke change. He took a deep drag of the cigarette, his thoughts going back to the ward.

What if he was moved, he'd be nothing, just a name, amongst a hundred others, no-one to influence there, just a face in the crowd. The only way to be noticed then would be through abnormal behaviour and that would be dealt with swiftly.

He lit a third cigarette and decided it was time to go...but which way? Along the canal, or back up the track? He reluctantly walked back up the track, only to be seen by the staff with the barrow gang who were returning to their wards for their meal.

A female (short stay) admission ward. In the early 1960's staff on the female ward were always women, and on the male wards only male nurses were allowed over 18 years old.

Chapter seven.

Manual work, other than nursing duties, was an accepted task for nurses of the sixties, and had been since the early days of the asylum. Nursing staff regularly delivered coal, chopped wood for sticks to light fires, and took out working parties of patients, to work in the fields or on the farm.

Most wards, except those with feeble, or extremely disturbed patients had an accepted role to play in ensuring the efficient, and effective running of the hospital, which was self sufficient for many of its needs.

Patients worked with the staff, in such places as the Laundry, Kitchens, Gardens and Shop. They grew some of their own fruit and vegetables, had two farms, tending their own animals, with herds of cattle and pigs. They also ran a battery hen farm, and made most of their own implements, as well as clothing and curtains.

What they bought in, ranging from shoes to furniture, they maintained and repaired themselves. In fact, there was a tinker, a tailor, and in occupational therapy you could become a candlestick maker.

There were patients employed in all these departments and work areas, in fact they were a vital part of the work force, in a lot of these specialities.

One building in the hospital was called Allentown, and also known as the brush shop. This was a prefabricated building, situated in the middle of the hospital, not far from the hospital church. Here the patients and staff made brushes, mats, and baskets. Some did woodwork, and made stools, tables and garden seats.

I was allocated to this department for three months, as a cadet nurse.

The people working in Allentown made the best yard brushes I've ever seen, strong and made to last. The ancillary staff, and the members of the barrow gang used them. They would sweep up everything before them with ease. They were always in demand as each ward was responsible for keeping the outside area as clean as the inside of the ward.

They also made sweeping brushes, scrubbing brushes, and clothes brushes all patiently by hand. Each brush head was held in a vice and the bristles were individually glued into each hole.

The glue was specially 'boiled up' by one of the patients and mixed to the thickness required for each size of brush. It used to bubble away on an old gas stove and the air was filled with its special smell.

The clothes brushes were real works of art, with fine bristles and a polished handle. Some of the patients in Allentown were skilled craftsmen, and spent most of their time away from the wards working at their specialities. They wore white aprons, and many wore sports coats, giving them an appearance different to the other patients, who worked. It was as if they were more than just an ordinary worker, they were craftsmen, and they acted like it.

I noticed that when they were concentrating on their work they rarely showed any of their symptoms of being mentally ill, and yet when they were away from Allentown, they were sometimes quite different, as if upset at being away from their work. Whatever it was, the effect of working in Allentown was certainly beneficial.

All types of mats were also made here, the majority being hard wearing coconut-type doormats which could be seen at every ward entrance.

I enjoyed working here and was able to learn a lot of new skills from the patients. I made a mat, helped restore some furniture, and painted some bird tables. I was aware that the patients treated me, and other cadets, not as nursing staff, but tolerated us, as if we were their apprentices, which I suppose we were.

Also I remembered when they had come to the barber's shop for a hair cut, they had made it clear with their body language, they wanted the barber, and not the apprentice cutting their hair.

It was becoming near the end of an era in self-sufficiency at the hospital, as discussions were taking place to buy some of these items in, rather than making them.

Plans were being discussed to change this area, which would be used for the introduction of an Industrial Therapy Unit. Patients would then be employed to fulfil contracts from outside agencies. And would be paid a small sum of money for their endeavours.

As a cadet I had been aware of the barrow gangs, having watched them work around the hospital grounds. They consisted of groups of male patients, supervised by staff (male nurses), and they pulled large carts, by long shafts, everywhere they went. The cart was often full of the brushes we made, together with shovels, rakes and pick axes. The gang varied in size according to its task, or from which ward it was located.

The largest barrow gang I had seen was from male Six. This ward had up to eighty patients on it at the time, and I was told that this was not the biggest for ward occupancy, as Male eight once had nearly 100 patients in it. Again like the brush shop, conventional therapies were beginning to change the function of these activities, and there were suggestions that the gangs changed to the more acceptable phrase of agricultural therapy. Another function of the brush shop was to occasionally take out smaller gangs, of unskilled patients to brush up leaves, and collect waste.

One of the most frustrating tasks I had was brushing up the leaves. There are a large number of trees in the grounds, especially magnificent horse chestnuts.

I never imagined the number of leaves that they would shed. If you were unlucky, the wind would blow down another lot of leaves, as one of the assistant chief male nurses came round, to inspect your work.

You could end up with a right telling off, as it appeared that you had done no work, although if they looked in the barrow, they could see you had. It was all part of the discipline, and grooming.

Other work in the hospital included small groups, or individuals, delivering coal or wood, around the wards, and to some of the offices, and buildings within the hospital. Delivering coal was an important role; especially to the female wards as some were three floors up in the 1829 building, which was at the front of the hospital. There were no lifts and it was a difficult task climbing up those spiral staircases. A more difficult task I was told was carrying corpses down those stairs, as they couldn't manoeuvre a stretcher around the twists and turns, so they had to be carried down manually. This was the nurses role as well. Fortunately the death rate was low on those wards, and patients were moved to a 'sick ward' if they became seriously ill. The female wards were a mystery to me. Although I had been in the hospital for two years, I had never been inside one, and they were as mystical to me, as they may be to an outsider. Sometimes when I passed one, I would hear an awful high-pitched scream, or hysterical laughter. On other occasions I would see these women in overcoats, walking around the airing courts, some putting their hands towards you through the railings, begging for a cigarette. To me they did look mad, somehow the look in their eyes was different, and I was intrigued by some of the tales the girl cadets told me about their behaviour. Some would allegedly scratch at your eyes, or pull your hair out, if they got hold of you in a rage. It was certainly acknowledged by some of the old hands that it was easier to restrain an angry man, than an angry woman, but I didn't intend to find out for myself.

Whatever work you did, be it nursing, or just painting a seat, the discipline was very strict. Everything was inspected to see if it was done properly. Not only was the discipline strict about your work, it was also strict for the cadets, regarding appearance and behaviour. On a Monday morning the male cadets would line up in the chief male nurse's office for inspection. This would include the crease in your trousers, your shoes, and especially your hair. The chief male nurse, an ex-navy man hated long hair, and surprisingly for a navy person, he would not allow beards.

If your hair was long he would 'lend' you the money until pay day, and send you to the Barber's shop in town. He forbid the hospital barber to cut our hair.

One cadet Dave, had long blond hair, and was sent twice to the barbers on the same day, only to return, with it still too long for the chief's satisfaction, so he was subjected to the ultimate penalty. He was sent to 'Big Tim', who was a charge nurse on the refractory ward. There he was held down with one hand and scalped with the other hand. Tim carried out his instruction in showing him what a haircut really was.

The cadet's soon started to cut each other's hair, borrowing the cutters from a ward. There were sometimes haircuts which the owner would rather not be seen with.

The discipline was necessary to keep us all in order and sometimes it was very severe. Some of the lads used to like a game of cards at break time, or sneak into a pub' for half a pint when going to college at lunchtime.

Two of us were reported for having been drinking and gambling, under age, a gross exaggeration. We were both given the choice of putting half of the £1 wages we received, after our keep had been taken out, into a post office account for three months, or leave the job. The chief bellowed at us, 'You won't be able to afford to drink when I have finished with you.'

*****

That walk to the canal, hastened Charlie's transfer, as he was reported for being out of bounds. Not only was he moved, but also his parole was stopped. All this happened the very next day.

'Pack up your things, and put them into this sack,' he was told. Then off he had gone, down

the ward without any goodbyes, and out into
the corridor, carrying the sack that contained
his only worldly possessions.

A nurse escorted him, carrying his case notes
and his money and watch in a valuables
envelope. He didn't even know where his new
ward was, until they crossed from the annexe
to the main part of the hospital. The corridors
here were long and dark, and patients hung
around in the gloom. Some were making
cigarettes on the window ledges, while others
were just there, a part of the place. Their
clothes were ill-fitting, and some wore trousers
that were half way up their legs. Charlie felt
frightened again, the same feelings came back
that he had experienced on his admission. In
spite of these emotions that were welling up
within him, he hadn't protested about his
move, and here he was meekly walking along
towards a place he was dreading, even
carrying his own belongings, over his shoulder
like some kind of pack animal.

He stopped abruptly as they neared the door
and threw the sack down. He didn't know who
was the more startled himself or the nurse.

'What's up with you?' the nurse asked abruptly.

'Pick that up and stop being stupid.'

'Stupid,' Charlie screamed as he came to his senses.

'It's you whose stupid if you think I am going in there with all those nutters,' he said, turning to walk away from the door.

The nurse grabbed his shoulder and pushed him against the wall, but Charlie was out of control. He kicked out, catching the nurse on the right shin, forcing him to let go of his shoulder.

Blinded by panic, and rage Charlie ran off. He ran up the dark corridor towards the light, the light he knew indicated the way out.

Reaching the exit, at the end of the corridor, he pushed through the doors and out into the grounds. The sudden glare from the light, and his sudden dash into the open, and public view, brought him back to his senses. Recovering from the shock of his unforeseen behaviour, he began to walk through the grounds and down towards the farm.

If I don't want to be noticed, I can't be seen hurrying, he reasoned. But where could he go? The staff were bound to be after him by now. The only way he knew was down to the canal and so that was where he headed, as fast as he dared.

'Hello Charlie,' cried a farmhand, unaware of his attempt to abscond.

'It's early for you to be out and about.'

'I'm taking a message to a nurse in the Willows,' Charlie replied without thinking, amazed at how his answer had come so easily. On he went, diverting to the canal track as soon as he could be reasonably sure he was out of sight.

Back in the corridor the nurse soon recovered from the shock he had received. He rang the ward doorbell and alerted the staff to Charlie's actions. His shin was sore and he was actually embarrassed about losing his patient, as this was seen by the other nurses as incompetence, even if they didn't actually say so.

The missing patient procedure was immediately put into action. The nurse in charge of the ward notified the senior nurse on duty, who instructed the staff from the ward to search the grounds.

When they reported back that they had not seen Charlie, the nurse in charge moved the missing patients' procedure on to its next stage.

Each ward was notified and nurses searched the area surrounding their own ward whilst other staff joined a search party in the grounds. Dr Minor's secretary was also informed, as was the head porter.

The grounds were systematically searched, including the outbuildings and bushes and staff were soon made aware that Charlie had been last seen heading towards the direction of the farm.

Back in the ward the nurse completed a written report of the incident and to diminish his own part of the escape added that Charlie had kicked him as he was putting the key into the ward lock, and that there had been no warning of the incident.

All patients' personal details are filed in the front of their case notes. The information included their physical characteristics, and any distinguishing marks, or behavioural traits. The information would be given to the police, if missing patients were not found within a time determined by their doctor, or nursing staff. This time limit was determined by the patient's history and as to whether they were suicidal, or a danger to themselves or others. Because of his 'violent' behaviour towards the nurse, Charlie was now deemed to be medium risk, although as this was thought to be an isolated incident the staff were given several hours to find him before any further action would be considered.

Reaching the canal bridge, Charlie leaned against the wall and looked back towards the hospital.

His chest hurt and he was breathing hard. He was not fit, smoked too much, and had spent most of his time in hospital lazing around when he wasn't doing his ward duties.

'You were fit enough to fight,' his conscience told him. 'You stupid fool.'

This was the very last thing he wanted himself to be thinking. His heart pounded faster and he wanted to be sick.

What had he done, and where should he go? Too late now to be sorry for his actions, he had to go, as far away as possible. So he moved on along the canal bank, trying to keep low and out of sight of the workers at the Willows. The staff there would soon be aware of him absconding.

He continued to feel nauseated from his physical exertions and also from thoughts of the consequence of his actions. He knew that when they found him he would be in serious trouble, especially for kicking the nurse, and this thought, and the fear of the inevitable enforced confinement, probably in the 'box', urged him on. The water in the canal seemed stagnant. Tall reeds and grasses grew at its edge and occasionally a moor-hen or heron would screech their alarm calls.

The canal bent to the right and beyond a small wood there was a large railway bridge, carrying the main Chester to Birkenhead line across the canal. On reaching the bridge Charlie scampered up the steep, slippery side and onto the track.

When he felt he was far enough away to be reasonably safe he hid in a small wood and rested against a tree, taking stock of his situation. In his pocket he found half a packet of Woodbines, a few matches, and two three-penny bits. Not much to survive on.

He lit one of his now precious cigarettes and let his thoughts wander back to why he had run away. He would not be here if they had left him alone, in the ward where he was happy, he kept thinking to himself. He had not wanted to be in hospital in the first place, it was them who had put him there and then, just as he was getting used to it, they were moving him to the long-stay patients, just for going for a walk away from the grounds. Well he had showed them, he was certainly away from the grounds now.

He'd show them who was mad!

Suddenly, he felt more lonely and dejected. Everything seemed hopeless and he began to cry. Then anger took over and more thoughts began to surface of his rejection by society. And so it went on, each thought followed by another, until his mind was swamped and he could hardly think rationally any more.

He also began to feel hungry and remembered his pills. No three meals a day, or medicine, round here. He no longer wanted to run and so he just sat down with his thoughts, getting colder and colder as the darkness took over, releasing him from those endless thoughts.

A police dog found him two days later, curled up in a ball, under a bush. He wasn't as far away as they had expected him to be and this had delayed his discovery.

He was cold, hungry, and weary and when they returned him to the ward and looking so dejected, he did not receive the aggravation he had anticipated.

He was bathed, checked over, and put into a side-room, not the pads, as he had expected. He was given a plastic mug of tea and two jam sandwiches and then left to sleep on a mattress placed on the floor. His medication was reviewed and again he was lucky as there would be no injections. He counted his blessings and slept.

He had only seen daylight when he was taken to the toilets where he was made to empty his pot and wash his hands and face. He was always thirsty and gulped down the water from the tap. The only change in the routine was that on the second day he was given a night-shirt instead of pyjamas.

When he was allowed up, he was surprised that a week had passed. They told him that he had been delirious, probably caught a fever, from sleeping rough. He was given antibiotics and daily drinks of Complan to supplement his meals and help put back the weight he had lost.

He remained in the ward, not allowed out, and his escape was soon just a few lines in the records, not unusual and not forgotten.

Charlie, one among many with not much to look forward to, was left to pick up the pieces of his restricted life.

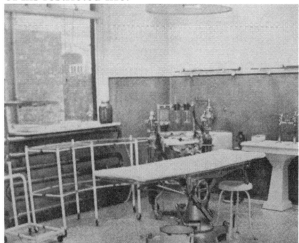

The operation theatre.

Chapter eight.

I could not believe how quickly three years had passed since I had started at the hospital. I had enjoyed my time as a cadet nurse and would miss my mates, but now that I had decided to make nursing my career, I was happy to leave them and start my training by moving onto the wards, I was eighteen years old and I was given a new contract as a student nurse. The training to become a Registered Mental Nurse (RMN) would take three years and a new national training syllabus was just being introduced.

I worked on a ward for the first time, a sick ward, for a period of eight weeks. This was to wait for the next training block to commence. I found this brief experience a great help in my preparation to start my education in Mental Nursing, it gave me some basic training skills and my first real contact with the patients.

I had come to know a lot of the patients as a cadet nurse, but now I was able to do hands on care, I eagerly read their case notes and became familiar with their illnesses.

I had also met a pretty nurse and was courting

strongly. She was a Welsh girl, who also lived in the nurses' home, so we saw each other most nights. She had recently started as a cadet nurse and travelled home only at the weekend, or on Bank Holidays. We went to the pictures, or the pub, and sometimes we walked by the river, or on the canal, down to the Willows. We were never allowed to officially visit each other's rooms.

A bonus in my new-found relationship was that she thought my shirts needed a proper ironing although I did feel a bit embarrassed at first, especially when she handed them back to me in front of my mates.

'You'll be getting married if you don't watch it,' they had jested.

The training school was not based at the Deva, but at Moston Hospital. The hospital was less than two miles up the road from where I worked and had opened in 1960, to relieve the pressure at the Deva Hospital. It was an old army hospital, made up of mostly wooden buildings, and the school was based at the back, near the staff houses.

There were twenty students in my class, some I knew, as they had been cadets with me, and others who had just started in the profession. Four of these were men from Tanganyika, Africa.

There were three classrooms and everyone sat behind desks, in four rows, just like we used to when we were at school. There were two tutors, and a practice nurse.

The daily timetable and training syllabus was explained and the senior tutor reminded us that we would have to study hard, if we were to pass our exams. He explained how it would sometimes be difficult to keep up with our studies when we would also be working on the wards full time. He especially emphasised that we should discipline ourselves and not rely on trying to cram everything into the last few weeks before an exam. He also mentioned about not working too much overtime on the wards.

I knew there was plenty of overtime available, with some nurses working two shifts in one day to supplement poor wages, and it was going to be a dilemma to turn down such an opportunity.

The tutor also mentioned sick leave. He told us that students were only allowed ten days each year and not to take off any odd days for minor ailments.

A handbook, published by the General Nursing Council, was circulated and this gave us all an in-depth knowledge about the training syllabus which covered three broad fields of study.

1. A systematic study of the human individual, both mind and body, relating normal development and behaviour, with the effects of mental disorder and physical illness.

2. The various skills in dealing with mental disorders, and bodily diseases associated with, or occurring in psychiatric patients.

3. Concepts of mental disorder, psychiatry and psychopathology.

The first six weeks of training were to be in the school of nursing, and then each student was given a list of their allocations to the different wards, and other specialities. We were informed that there would be further 'blocks'
(weeks) of teaching to attend at the training school, with two major examinations to pass. The first would be the intermediate examination; covering those parts of the

syllabus included in the first year of training, and would be taken at the end of the first year. The final examination covered the whole of the syllabus and would be taken after three years. There were also hospital examinations in written and practical form, and each one would have to be passed.

I soon found the advantage of having been a cadet; it gave me a good start as we studied for our G.C.E.s in anatomy and physiology, at the college of further education. I had also learned some of the practical nursing skills, such as bed-making, and setting up various trays and trolleys.

During lunch breaks I explored Moston Hospital with some of the other students. When we walked around the corridors, I saw that we were actually walking through the centre of the wards which were named after trees, such as Beech, Cherry, Durian, Elm, Fir. The hospital had been unkindly christened the 'Doll's Hospital' by some of the staff from down the road, because it was made of wood and was said to be the place for those who had suffered a nervous breakdown, as it did not have the stigma of the Deva, which was where you went if you were mad.

During our training, we were taught that Moston was in advance of most hospitals in the country, as it incorporated a Day Hospital, an Adolescent Unit and a pioneering Alcoholic Dependency Unit. There was a rivalry with the Deva staff because of the way Moston had developed and I always remembered what a charge nurse had told me when the teasing began.

'They always send to the Deva the cases they can't handle, such as the one's with unpredictable behaviour, like the violent and suicidal,' This was right, as they hadn't the secure facilities at Moston. Sometimes the same rule applied to 'difficult' staff.

*****

Charlie did not know how long he had been 'stuck' in his new ward and was shocked when the staff arranged for a cake to be made by the hospital pastry cook, to celebrate his twenty-first birthday. He had not realised it was his birthday. Unfortunately, the day soon passed and he was back into the dreary routine of the ward. Each day after breakfast, he and the other patients were allowed to wash and shave under the general supervision of a nurse who did little more than hurry them up, to relieve the congestion of the packed wash-room. There was a large dirty roller towel on the wall, and it was covered in bloodstains, from shaving cuts. Charlie struggled to find a clean bit to dry his face on, though it didn't really bother him, as he had passed caring.

Later, those who did not have work chores were sent out into the airing court, a large garden area, with a bowling green in the centre. A concrete path ran around the outer perimeter, on which most of the patients trudged along. Most walked with their heads down, arms slumped by their side, walking in a slow monotonous pace. Still walking to nowhere, to do nothing, to see no-one. Just walking round and round, sometimes moved on by the escorting nurses, who were usually the junior members of staff.

There were benches to sit on if the weather was fine, and simple gardening tasks, such as weeding, or brushing up leaves, which kept some of the patients occupied.

The flower-beds were neatly kept in the centre and corner of the lawns, and large trees, including a splendid horse chestnut tree, graced the area.

The trees provided plenty of work in the autumn, as the outside of the ward had to be kept as clean as the inside, and the staff were still chastised if the wind brought a fresh load of leaves down just before the Chief male nurse's inspection.

Charlie was glad to get outside and into the fresh air. Just to smell that air, free of cigarette smoke, and body odour.

Fresh air was a precious commodity when you lived in such close proximity of so many people, he thought. Not that he was exactly alone outside, as half the ward was with him. To access the airing court, the patients were marched along the side of the ward and through a large gate, which was locked when the last one was in. It amused Charlie how patients reacted when they got there. Some went right, some left, while others just stood still and yet within five minutes, those walking around the court, were all going the same way. Charlie was becoming good at such observations. He was now also beginning to tell the events of the ward by their smell, another habit he had developed when trying to relieve his boredom, a habit that was fast becoming an obsession.

Each one was different and, when he was walking around, he would close his eyes and imagine a different environment by its smell. They were not always smells he could describe to someone else, but identifiable to himself when an area or ward was mentioned. They actually described the personality of the ward when different nurses were in charge.

There were smells of polish, Brasso or carbolic soap. He associated these with authority, from his own childhood, when he was doing his chores, or with staff who had the patients cleaning all day.

The smell of paraldehyde lingered on the breath of patients who were on this sleeping draught. Charlie found its smell distasteful, and it always seemed to come from patients who talked into your face, coming into your personal space as he called it. A number of patients had become addicted to paraldehyde and could not function properly without it.

Charlie knew of a patient on the ward who actually bought a draught of the stuff from another patient. He had seen him shake the bottle before he took the cork off and little bubbles had formed in the draught. The patient had then put the bottle to his mouth and gulped it all down.

Charlie also said that he could tell when something was going to 'brew up' as he called it. He thought of this as the smell of fear, and this usually heralded a rough house. This was more of a feeling he had developed from previous incidents.

He could smell the meals. The laundry, the toilets, the hall, everything, he had even added noises to his repertoire. All this was further distancing him from reality in one sense, but in another sense, it was actually bringing him closer to the environment he increasingly loathed.

The pleasanter smells were the smell of breakfast coming down the corridor from the kitchen, bacon and tomatoes today, he would say, or not butter beans again, which he hated. But his favourite smell was wood burning or shag tobacco. He could not smoke the stuff as some of the patients did, but he simply loved the smell of it.

Today, when leaving the ward, he had smelled furniture polish, and as he was walking around the airing court, his mind had gone back to when as a child he would sit and watch his granny polish the furniture.

She would rub the polish into the table and then bring it to a shine with a clean cloth. He marvelled at such energy for an old lady in her eighties, but he had never appreciated her age as a child and just expected her to be immortal. She used to tell him stories when she was working. His favourite was when she was scrubbing the kitchen floor. She would say that the soapsuds were the Germans, who were the enemy. Then she would rinse her cloth, in a bucket of clean water, and tell him that here comes the British to wipe them away, rinsing the soapsuds away.

He had not realised who these Germans were, but he knew they were the 'baddies' by his granny's demeanour. A sudden frown crossed his face as his memory turned to another incident that interrupted his pleasant state of reverie. It was when his granny was trying to polish out a scratch in the table which he had made with his penknife.

'I told you not to sharpen your pencil on the table,' she had said. She had always protected him, him being the eldest of five children, and he in turn had worshipped her. But he had already known what he would get when his mother came home from work, whether his granny was there or not. A kicking if he sat down or a whipping if he stood up. No holds barred when she started. Then up to bed for the rest of the day without any meals; he wouldn't risk going down to the toilet, which was outside, as she would start again, so he often spent most of the night in misery.

The worse part for him was the lies he would be forced to tell afterwards.

'Fell over again, Charlie,' his teacher would say, in that knowing voice.

'No Miss, walked into a door,' he would reply, head down, and shamed-faced.

Then there was the lecture she gave him when she realised what she had done. There was never an apology, she just sought justification. 'It's only for your own good,' she would say. 'It's not easy bringing up five children without a father.'

Charlie's pace quickened as he came out of his thoughts. Faster and faster he would go until he nearly knocked the others down.

'At it again Charlie,' shouted the nurses who attributed his behaviour to him hearing the 'voices'.

Charlie never replied, he didn't even hear them. He was not walking to nowhere, he was walking onwards.

On his better days, Charlie didn't see himself as being obsessed with smells and tried to discuss them with those who would listen.

One patient who had been to prison told him that he could identify areas there, in the same way as Charlie could, especially with noise. He told him that he was able to imagine what was going on outside his cell, even when he couldn't see anything that was happening. He just got used to the noise of the different events.

This fascinated Charlie, so he started to close his eyes, and concentrate on the noises of the ward. There was nothing else to occupy him anyway, he thought.

He became aware that some of the patients

muttered to themselves all day, something he hadn't really noticed before.

Others were silent, they never said a thing on their own volition, only replying to questions when asked. There were times you could hear a pin drop, on the ward, other times it was like bedlam.

Concentrating on the staff, Charlie became more aware of their personalities, something else he had not really thought about before. Some screamed at you, some were polite, some sang or whistled all day, others said very little.

The sounds of the meals arriving always fascinated him. A game he played, if he was in the mood, was to close his eyes, and anticipate the meal arriving. Waiting to see if the first hint was a sound or a smell.

What came first to his senses to tell him it was dinner-time? The sound or the smell?

If it was fish, it was usually the smell. If it was a roast, it was the sound, usually tin lids banging as a member of the staff hijacked its arrival, to pinch a chunk of meat while the charge nurse's back was turned.

On the ward the deputy charge nurse would

not let them commence eating until everyone was silent, including the staff. A remarkable achievement when you consider there was over eighty mad men on the ward. The same rule was applied when the meal was over. No one left the table until there was complete silence. When this was attained he would bellow, 'Stand up all.' Charlie had heard him say to a young member of staff, 'That made them jump'.

It hadn't, as the alert patients were used to this regular nonsense, whist the rest were too involved in their own thoughts and didn't even hear him.

Closing his eyes and listening, Charlie's obsession with sound continued. The chairs scraping across the floor, tables moving, petty squabbles as neighbour's water or bread was being stolen. Then there was the staff chasing the stragglers to their tables, with rebukes for the latecomers, so that the head count could be done, as everybody had to be present and correct. Then there was the cough, the shout, the clip on the ear, the belch, the fart all breaking the silence required for us to be allowed to eat. And then the smell of the meal that was coming, fish and chips, pie or scouse, not really very hard to guess, as the meals were usually the same for each day of the week. Friday was Charlie's favourite, fish and chips, the best he had ever tasted.

The nurses stood behind the food wagon, in line of seniority to serve the meals. The senior was always on the meat, then the vegetables and potatoes, with the junior on the gravy, or serving, then collecting the dirty dishes. Sometimes a patient assisted the staff.

'No peas nurse,' somebody shouted.

'Shut up, and get them down you,' had been the reply. Charlie had noticed that the meals were sometimes served according to the pecking order of the ward, like everything else. The favoured and the feared, got the bigger meals, and seconds, the despised and naughty got less.

'Full patients can't fight, they sleep,' a nurse had once told him.

A pudding always followed dinner. There was sponge and custard, or rice, with a blob of jam in the middle, always a favourite.

The utensils were cleared up at the end of the meal and the kitchen men would start to wash up.

Charlie and the others received their medication whilst they were all sitting down, as the nurses could never cope if they all started moving around, such were the numbers and confusion. On those days when the deputy was on duty, they still had to wait for the minutes silence, otherwise they just got up table by table.

After each meal, Charlie and the other patients who smoked formed a queue outside the charge nurse's office, waiting for the cigarettes or tobacco to be given out. Those without would hang around him and pester him to death for a 'fag' or a stump. This always ruined his smoke, so like some of the others, he would seek a quiet hideout, somewhere in the ward.

Some of the patients were not allowed matches, so they used a small gas flame that was situated in the corner of the day room. The rest just slept.

After lunch was finished, the staff had their meals and then their smoke. Most stayed on the ward, part of the fixtures. They would sit next to the door, if the boss hadn't been

around, so that they could see him coming, otherwise they would sit with the patients. Even the staff who smoked were not left in peace to enjoy it, as the scroungers hung around ready to grab their stumps when they were discarded. Once they were rested it was down the 'backs' to use the toilet for the patients and then to the airing court for Charlie and the others...
and around they would walk until teatime.

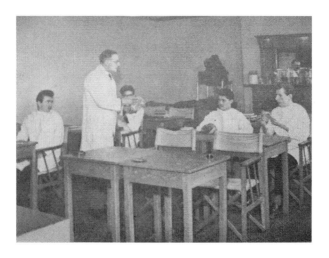

An anatomy lesson by the head tutor, Mr Nutter.

The Deva Hospital nurse training school, approved by the General Nursing Council for the complete training of men and women as mental nurses. The school moved to Moston Hospital in the 1960's.

Chapter nine.

My next ward as a student nurse was Male 2, better known to the staff as '*Shit Alley*', and it didn't take me long to find out why. I unlocked the ward door with my pass key and the smell hit me immediately. It was not that I hadn't become accustomed to bad smells, but this smell was especially bad, in fact it was terrible.

My first sight of the patients was a bigger shock to my system than the smell. They were all classed as 'subnormal' or 'severely subnormal' and a more bizarre bunch of characters I would never meet again, staff or patients.

I felt quite threatened at first as the patients were noisy, boisterous and some were severely deformed. The staff didn't help much either. There was no induction here, just an almost sadistic delight in watching how I would react to this almost macabre experience.

New staff were judged on how they reacted to this, a very startling experience for them, and all the other different situations they would encounter. It all added up as to how they would be accepted, especially for people like myself, who had no family employed at the hospital.

The most deformed man in the ward was a man called Cedric. He came towards me with his mouth hung open and long strings of slobber dribbled out. Half his nose was missing and this gave the impression that you could see almost into the inside of his head. His arms were contracted up to his chest and he walked on the tip of his toes, with a limp.

I felt both scared and embarrassed as I didn't know how I would react towards him. I didn't want him to touch me on this my first day, but if we didn't touch each other, how was I going to nurse him? Certainly not by the non touch technique.

I noticed that the poor fellow was smiling at me and the thought ran through my mind that Cedric didn't think himself as being any different to myself, and neither should he, so I took him by the arm and sat him down in a chair and wiped his face with a towel.

I soon learned how to love him, as I would most of the other characters on Male two. They were dependent on the staff and in their different ways all seemed to demand affection. Although designated for patients who were classed as being subnormal, the ward also catered for patients who had contracted infectious diseases such as typhoid fever and dysentery. Most of these had suffered from one, or more, of these diseases during their stay in hospital which, in their cases, was usually for the rest of their lives. There was nowhere else for them to go.

There were almost fifty patients on this ward, one of the smaller wards in the long-stay part of the hospital. This was because of the high dependency of the patients which made the workload very heavy and demanding.

The morning shift, which started at 7am, had four or five staff. One was the charge nurse or his deputy, two would be student nurses, and the others were assistant nurses.

One of the assistant nurses who never seemed to be off-duty was a man called Joe. He was middle-aged and I was told that he was French, although you couldn't really tell as he rarely spoke to anybody. Sometimes he would whisper the odd word, usually to take over an unpleasant task, such as cleaning up an

incontinent patient. Joe did this with most of
the staff as, apparently, he saw this to be his
role. Bathing, toileting, cleaning,...he hardly
stopped working all day.
When he did stop he would never join the rest
of the staff for a break. Instead he would stand
in a corner of the ward, scribbling away into a
notebook that he carried everywhere.
Everybody was curious to know what he wrote
down.
I wondered at first how he could have possibly
got a job here with his unusual mannerisms,
later I appreciated that when he was off duty
he was really missed.
As a student nurse, I was not treated any
differently than the rest of the staff and was
expected to be part of the ward team. I had to
learn quickly and was expected to take charge
of the ward for short periods of time, when the
others were on their break.
We started the day with a cup of tea, usually
'stewed' from being left on the cooker by the
kitchen man who had made it. It was always
dark and strong, 'strong enough for the spoon
to stand up in it,' one of the nurses had said.
Because of the amount of infection on the

ward, I was warned that it was not unusual to get a bout of the 'trots' as this was normal for most new staff.

I was also told that I would soon become immune, which I did, especially when I realised that the crockery was 'colour coded'. Anything with a green rim around it was for the infected patients and was from the dysentery kitchen which was separate from the main ward kitchen.

The first task of the day was to get the patients up and prepare them for their breakfast. They slept in one of two dormitories or in a side room. Some patients were able to get themselves up, and two of them even assisted the staff, such was the variety of the mix of patient on here.

One of the patients was a man called Joey Kirt, better known as 'Shit Kirt'. The other patient's name was Eddie Flower, known as, 'Soft shoe shuffle Flower'. Everyone seemed to have a nickname here.

Joey got his name for two reasons, firstly because he walked around shouting, 'Shit kirt', a habit he had learned from the staff over many years. They would shout this to him every time they found anything which Joey would be expected to remove with his rag. The second reason was from the rag itself. This was filthy and was not only used to pick up offending objects.

Eddie Flower, on the other hand, thought he had more class than the other patients and I really did wonder what he was doing on this ward. He had acquired his nickname from his shuffling style of dancing at the weekly patients' dance. He really was the Fred Astaire of the hospital and he even wore black patent shoes.

Once all the patients were up in a morning they were put into chairs, or taken to the table for their breakfast. Some were tied with a sheet, which went around their waist and the back of their chair, to prevent them from falling out.

I helped feed several of them, giving them bread and milk, which was the choice of diet for most of these patients. Because of their handicaps, most were unable to feed themselves. I soon found that it was an aquired skill to feed them. Some just opened their mouths wide and waited for the next spoonful to go in, whilst others had to be coaxed as they turned their faces when when you tried to put the spoon in their mouth. Another would lash out, covering us both with breakfast, and when it was noticed that I had more breakfast on the patient's lap than in his mouth, I was quickly reminded to put on the plastic aprons, or bibs. I was told that the patients' clothing was sometimes difficult to acquire due to the amount being used so I would put underclothes, or pillow-cases around their necks if no bibs were available. I was also told that the patients needed regular toileting, after each meal and before going to bed. Following the first toileting session, which followed breakfast, the patients were either taken to sit down in the day room, or if the weather was fine, taken out into the airing court.

Fred and Joey, together with some of the patients who could feed themselves, were given a cooked breakfast and when they were not helping out on the ward were allowed out into the grounds.

When I thought that we had finished getting up all the patients I was told that my next task was to assist with care in the side rooms. The patients here were more disturbed and they were the last to be got up. They had to be under continual observation and were 'slopped' out and washed. Slopping out, I soon discovered, meant collecting their rubber pots (if they were the right way up) and emptying them.

I was then shown how to open the window shutters which were necessary to prevent the patients from harming themselves. The bedding always seemed to be wet and this had to be changed and the room mopped out. Some of the patients slept on mattresses laid on the floor, covered with thick bed linen. This was necessary because of a patients' destructive behaviour. Some of them would tear or break everything they came in contact with.

A few patients at night wore a type of boiler suit, designed so that they could not get out of it on their own. I was told that these patients would harm themselves if they did not wear them. This was usually by some form of self-mutilation, like severe scratching, or putting objects into their body orifices.

One patient was unable to mix with the rest of the ward population due to his behaviour. It

was another shock for me to come into contact
with someone who had no social skills at all
and only communicated by grunting. He put
everything he could grab into his mouth and
was classed as being severely subnormal with
a concentration level of seconds. This patient
was also very agile and dived to pick up
anything he could...rubbish, insects (usually
cockroaches), leaves and even cigarette stubs.
I was shocked at the stories staff told me about
him. It was impossible to do anything to
improve his lifestyle. He could not be left
alone for a minute on the ward, though he was
allowed to go out in a fenced-off area of the
airing court.

Student nurses were allocated to each ward for
three months and after a few days I settled
down and got used to the routine. I had already
consented to work extra hours as it was hard to
refuse, seeing how short of staff they were.
I soon learned the patients' names, and their
little mannerisms, and became comfortable
working on the ward.

I was still disturbed at the different levels of
ability the patients had. Some were completely
dependent on the staff and that was why they

were here. But there was one or two who were quite the opposite, practically capable of being independent, with some supervision. They were capable of working on the ward, running messages to the shop and they went to church, the pictures or the dance and even had a bet on the horses.

The bets were placed with a bookies' runner, himself a patient, who took the written bets to town on odd bits of paper. He could always be found each day in the same place, in the corridor at lunchtime using a window-sill as a shelf. He was small, grey haired with glasses. He usually wore a jacket that had bulging pockets, probably from the coins and bets he kept in them. He took the bets from both staff and patients and paid out any winnings the next day. The bosses sometimes placed a bet with him, usually on the Derby or Grand National. He was another patient in the hospital who was a law unto himself, as he did very much as he pleased.

He said very little to the patients who bet with him, but I found him to have quite a sense of humour. Once when placing a bet with him he said, '

'You can see why I am going mad', and showed me a bet from a long-stay patient. Sixpence win on a horse at 10-1 on!

There seemed no logical reason to me why the independent type of patients were on this ward and it bothered me. I queried it with the staff and was told that the justification seemed to be the same on many of the wards. If a patient appeared to be getting better, assuming they were ill in the first place, tough luck, not good luck for them. There was little acknowledgement of any improvement, other than perhaps an extra workload which was at least appreciated by the staff from whom they took over the additional chore. There was certainly no chance of a discharge or even a transfer to a better ward for, as I was often told, a good patient is always replaced with a bad one and we've got enough of them already.

'*Shit Alley*' had a long corridor which stretched between the dormitories and the day room, with the sanitary annexe situated half the way down it.

The corridor had to be kept clean, as did the entire ward, and I quickly learned that, as there were no cleaners employed for the wards, it had to be cleaned by the nursing staff, who were sometimes assisted by the patients.

The task I found to be quite an art. The tools for the job, I was told, were a squeegie (a large implement to push away the water); a scrubbing brush on a stale (called a deck scrubber), a bumper and the fire hose. A bumper was a large block, hinged onto a large polished stale, making it manoeuvrable, and it was used to polish the floor.

The procedure was to throw a bucket of soapy water down the corridor, scrub it, rinse it down with the fire hose, push the water out of a door with the squeegie and then let it dry. Cover the floor when dry, with wax (sometimes the next day) and then polish it with an old cloth placed underneath the bumper.

Now this is where I found the art came in. Firstly, you got a number of patients, or a junior member of staff, to walk up and down the corridor. They pulled the bumper up and down, until there was some resemblance of a shine on the floor. Then you could concentrate on small areas and this was when the 'volunteers' stepped in, as the art was to push and pull the bumper in different ways. This I soon learnt was a very effective way of body building.

First pull with one hand, then the other, backwards, forwards, sideways, through the legs and so on. There was even a set of exercises for the different muscle groups, such as the 'pecs' and the 'lats', (slang for chest and back muscles). These exercises were continued until the floor shone like glass.

A long roller carpet was then put down the middle of the corridor, which made the place look quite respectable.

One day, when Joe was having one of his quieter moments and writing in his notebook, a patient fell, cutting his eyebrow quite badly. In the ensuing panic, as the wound was bleeding quite profusely, Joe rushed to the patient's aid, leaving his notebook on the windowsill.

When the emergency was over Joe returned to his spot in the ward, only to find the notebook missing. He searched around frantically, looked in patients' pockets but could not find it. He remained agitated for most of that day, but never asked any members of staff whether they had seen it. Most only found out what was wrong when the book was produced in the staff room at tea time. One of the nurses had taken it, borrowed it as he said, but he would only let Joe find it again when he had seen what was written in the notebook. Stupidly he accused Joe of being a management spy. What a shock he got when he eventually read it contained Joe's thoughts about some of the patients. It was very touching.

It was written in English, but some of it was in French. Without thinking I said that I had done some French at school and so, under pressure from my peers, was given the task of reading it.

It began by describing some of the physical characteristics of a patient, together with his mental and physical handicaps. It then basically said things such as:

'Although this patient looks deformed to me, he sees himself as normal, as most of us think we are. This is because he is normal, as that is what it is like, to be John. There is no other way he could be, if he didn't look like he does, he would no longer be John'.

Then there was a passage, which contained some criticism of the staff's attitude towards that patient.

It continued: 'Men are not only flesh and bones; men are also what they think they are. John is seen crippled and bent by us, but John sees us as straight and tall, so that's how John may see himself.'

'He may also think differently to how I have heard them say how he thinks. Although classed as simple, that may be because they don't know how to communicate with him, he may be locked up inside himself, unable to get out, so in his frustration he throws himself about the floor.'

Then we were shocked and ashamed by the next passage. It said, 'In the camp, I saw men end up like John, become bent and mute, due to their fear, and torment. It was soon forgotten that they were intelligent beings, and they were soon regarded and treated as imbeciles.'

There was a silence amongst us all. What right had we to pry into someone else's private life, without any thought for the consequences? Afterwards a new respect was shown towards Joe.

I enjoyed my time on Male 2 and once I had learned all the patients names and diagnosis, I felt comfortable within myself working there.

I learnt that most of the patients on this ward were classed as being subnormal, or severely subnormal. Definitions of these terms were outlined in the Mental Health Act of 1959. The charge nurse explained that those classified as subnormal had an I.Q. (Intelligence Quotient) of between 50 and 70, and the severe subnormal had I.Q.'s below 50. A lot of these patients also had severe physical disabilities as well, such as deafness, blindness, and lameness.

I tried to remember the advice our tutor had given us, and study whilst on the wards. I read some of the case notes, seeking out histories and diagnosis. Some of the notes were over 40 years old and were very thick and battered in appearance. Some classified the patients as being imbeciles and I came across conditions such as Cretinism, Microcephaly, and G.P.I. (General Paralysis of the Insane). There were several patients on the ward diagnosed as having the condition called G.P.I., and also Tabes Dorsalis. Another was said to have Congenital Syphilis. I understood that these terms were related so I decided to study them in more detail, as they had both mental and physical symptoms.

The charge nurse told me that G.P.I. was caused by a syphilitic infection affecting the brain, and advised me to read about Neurosyphilis from my textbook.

I knew that Syphilis was a venereal disease, but had never been aware that it could cause such terrible symptoms, years after the primary infection.

I read that a small corkscrew like organism, which was called a spirochaete, (treponema pallidum), was conveyed during sexual intercourse, by direct contact from an infected person to the partner. When it enters the body it circulates in the blood stream and so gains access to all parts. In a minority of cases it attacks the nervous system. Causing a condition known as neurosyphilis.

Neurosyphilis is seen in three main forms according to which part of the nervous system is affected. Some patients may present features of two or three forms.

Cerebral or Meningovascular Syphilis occurs when the meninges and the blood vessels supplying the central nervous system are affected. The commonest symptoms are headache, lethargy, and paralysis of eye movement, transient weakness of limbs, Fits and confusional attacks.

Tabes Dorsalis, which affected the patient's gait (ataxia), and this condition was once known as Locomotor Ataxia. I had already observed this unusual gait on the ward with the patient walking in a high stepping type of action. The charge nurse showed me the pupils of his eyes, and said he had what was known as Argyll Robertson pupils. He further explained that the pupils became small, irregular in shape and unequal, and that they react to accommodation, but not to light. This meant that they would contract or dilate when looking at near or far objects respectively, but not otherwise.

I learned that General Paralysis of the Insane occurred when the brain substance is affected by the syphilitic infection and is the type of neurosyphilis of most psychiatric importance. I was surprised to find that it manifests itself in a proportion of those infected by syphilis, some fifteen to twenty years after the primary genital lesion.

The clinical picture was one of slow

progressive dementia. Symptoms included emotional instability, depression, grandiose delusions, epilepsy, and Argyll Robertson pupils were common. It all seemed downhill for the patient to me, with incontinence and maybe spasticity of the limbs. It was a progressive mental and physical deterioration and we had several G.P.I. Patients on the ward. 'All that for going with one woman,' the charge nurse joked.

On a more serious note he warned me about not letting myself come in contact with an infected patient's blood and, afterwards, I was always wary about cutting them when I gave them a shave. A special blood test was done called a Wasserman and Kahn test. If it returned as positive, the person was infected.

I was amazed how much there was to learn about one condition and wondered how much I would have to know to pass my future exams.

I was beginning to see how mental and general nursing was fitting together, as many of the mental illnesses had physical signs and symptoms.

I was having difficulty with the abbreviations. It was like a new language but again I was

benefiting from having been a cadet nurse. I had learned the blood tests in the Path Lab and I had picked up the abbreviations needed to give out drugs whilst working in the Pharmacy...the likes of
t.d.s. (three times a day), and nocte, (at night). Those three years as a cadet nurse had certainly been valuable. I had come to know a lot of the staff and some of the patients and this helped me settle down quickly in my new working environment.

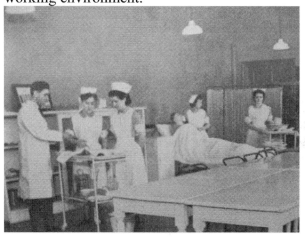

Nurses had to pass hospital and national intermediate exams before they were allowed

to enter the second year of training.
At the end of the third year they had to pass a
hospital practical and written exam and the
final R.M.N.
(Registered Mental Nurse examination).

Chapter ten.

Charlie was sitting in the day room the day
Jack collapsed and died. It was totally
unexpected and left those who could
understand very shocked and frightened.
Jack was a big man, not exceptionally tall, but
big around the waist, so that his clothes never
seemed to fasten around his stomach. The
button on his jacket always seemed to be
straining, as if ready to fly off at the first
opportunity.
Jack seemed to be part of the furniture on the
ward, as he had been there for years. He was a
middle-aged man and had a red face which
seemed to get redder and redder when he
became agitated. This was when he was
disturbed by the 'voices', which he would
answer. Sometimes he burst out laughing for
no apparent reason, and other times he would
slap himself across the head shouting, 'bugger
off', 'bugger off', as if he was trying to stop
hearing their daily torment.
The rest of the time he spent just sitting down,
and smoking, as he never bothered with
anybody else.

This day, he had got up from his chair in the crowded day-room, having just woken up from his after-dinner snooze. He had a cigarette in his mouth and was heading for the gas lighter in the corner of the room when he collapsed. He just crashed down to the floor, making a sighing noise as he fell.

A patient rushed out of the room to fetch a nurse and Charlie thought he must have had a fit, which was not uncommon on the ward. The only thing that nagged at him, and he knew the symptoms as well as the staff did, was that Jack was not a known epileptic.

Jack hadn't moved since he collapsed. He was frothing at the mouth and blood was running from a deep cut in his scalp and he started to wet himself.

Some of the patients got up from their chairs and began to leave the room.

This always amazed Charlie and he wondered if it was an act of showing respect for the afflicted, or was it just fear, or even indifference?

Charlie stayed where he was, sitting at the top of the day-room, and watched. Two nurses arrived and rolled Jack onto his back. Jack's eyes appeared glazed and he didn't seem to be breathing. A nurse was checking for a pulse and he heard the other confirm that Jack wasn't breathing. An oxygen cylinder was brought and a mask placed over his face. Other staff arrived and Jack was carried away to the dormitory.

The first indication that Jack had died came from the nursing staff. They closed off the dormitory area and the doctor was seen to arrive and leave soon afterwards. This was always a clue, Charlie reckoned. If a doctor made only a brief visit to a seriously ill patient, there was nothing he could do but confirm he was dying or dead.

The ward became very quiet. Nobody seemed to move. Charlie thought that the patients seemed to 'sober up,' and get temporarily better. As if shocked out of their madness by the sudden death of a fellow patient, they did not present their symptoms. This quietness persisted until well after the staff had taken Jack's body from the ward. One of the patients had mopped up the bloodstains from the floor and everyone sat around reminded of their own mortality.

Charlie felt really shocked. Not that he had any special feelings towards Jack, he hardly knew him. It was the suddenness of it all. One minute he was there and the next minute he was dead. There had been no warning, no indication he was ill. He certainly wasn't old and if it could happen to Jack it could happen to any of them.

Charlie had thought, from time to time, about dying...usually when he felt low. He could never forget the night he had woken up trembling, when he was a young child, realising that he was not immortal and that one day he would die. That fear had not really left him but it had not crossed his mind recently. He didn't want to die on this ward, especially now he had seen how cheap death seemed here.

The staff had done everything they could and they had been efficient and respectful. It was just not the place to die.

His memory drifted back to the time his grandfather had died in the front room. He had been ill for a while and his bed had been moved downstairs. Charlie used to sit on his bed, as in their small living room there was such little space for all the family to gather during the evenings. The children were normally sent to bed early to relieve the pressure.

At first it disturbed him that his grandfather was dying, but sometimes he became annoyed and sickened by the noises and smells that came from his bed. There was no inside lavatory and his grandfather, suffering from cancer of the bowel, had to be put on the pot which was usually too late, anyway. The smell hung in the room, and the night he died everyone was sitting around waiting for it to happen. Charlie sat at the back of the room, moving only to put the kettle on, to make the endless cups of tea, or open the door to callers. He sat there listening to his grandfather's breathing which went faster and faster and then stopped.

'He's gone,' somebody said, and the room was silent. As Charlie glanced up to see, his grandfather took a deep noisy breath and everyone seemed to jump up startled. Charlie nearly collapsed with fright and he was glad to have been told to go to bed, 'as it was no place for a child'.

The next morning his grandfather had gone. Charlie didn't go to the funeral he just got on with his life.

Charlie had been sitting near to Jack for several years but realised that his emotions were selfishly for his own feelings. He wouldn't really miss him, or any other patient who was moved or died. You couldn't afford to attach yourself to anyone here because it could become too painful. This summed up his feelings for the ward and the staff...everything about the place in fact.

He knew from experience that once the shift changed, everything would be back to the normal routine and the records would show just another empty bed.

This thought certainly shook him and so he got up and headed for the toilets, where he always went when he wanted to be alone.

Later, on returning to the day-room, Charlie saw that the next reaction to the shock of Jack's sudden death was occurring. One of the patient's had sat in another patient's chair and a petty squabble had turned into a major fight. The staff waded in, as if glad to release their own feelings and anxieties, and all hell was let loose.

Charlie made himself scarce, again returning to the toilet area. He sat on the toilet and blew smoke from his cigarette, watching it drift towards the ceiling. He was safely locked in his memories until, about an hour later, the nurse opened the door and told him his tea was ready. He returned to an almost normal environment and still cynical he commented that the only sign of Jack's departure was his vacant chair at the tea table.

*****

During my research into the history of the hospital I had come across a Chester County Asylum report dated 1879. In it was a report about the death, and post mortem of a 75-year-old woman. This became of special interest to me as I was toying with the idea of attending a post mortem. Some of the nurses in my group at the school had been and one was boasting about it.

Rising to the challenge, I asked the charge nurse on the ward if I could go and see one in the mortuary. I told him that it was for learning purposes, but I didn't sound very convincing. The charge nurse, probably guessing why I really wanted to go, said that I would learn very little at this stage of my training and asked me was it really for my own morbid curiosity. I insisted it was for my own experience and so it was arranged.

The mortuary was situated at the front of the hospital, next to the gardening department, and was known as Ivy Cottage.

It was the duty of ward staff to take the bodies to the mortuary if the death had been on their ward. The nurses would lay the dead person out on their bed, usually an hour after death. One nurse told me they waited an hour to give respect and time for the soul to leave the body. They would then wash and shave the corpse and pack the orifices to stop any leaking. They would see that any teeth were put in and then tie a bandage around the head and under the jaw to keep the mouth closed. Damp cotton wool balls would be placed over the eye lids to keep the eyes closed and finally, a shroud would be put on. Rings would be removed or left on according to the relatives wishes, and the body would be transferred by trolley, to the mortuary.

Inside the mortuary there were several rooms. The main one was where the post mortems were carried out, with a specially designed table in the centre of it. Large sinks and cupboards, for the instruments and bowls were on the side, and measuring and weighing equipment, such as scales, were on a table close by.

Another room contained a large refrigerator where the bodies were stored.

There was also a chapel where the body was put for viewing by any relatives who wished to see their loved one. In some cases the chapel was used for identifying people, as bodies were brought in by the police from road traffic accidents and suspicious deaths.

A purple sheet, with a gold cross on it would cover the body and a wooden cross was sited at the head of the trolley. The chapel was designed to help give a feeling of peace to those who came to see their departed. The other rooms were for storage and toilet purposes.

I had been to the mortuary on several

occasions with a body from the wards, so I was familiar with the environment. On this visit I was extremely apprehensive as I made my way to see my first post mortem. One of the older members of the nursing staff was assisting the pathologist and the body of an elderly male was naked on the examination table. Fortunately I did not recognise him. With the pathologist was a policeman in the background, the coroner's constable. They appeared relaxed and were just chatting to each other, although they paused to acknowledge me when I entered.

The older nurse, Rob, had often told staff on the wards tales of what had gone on at different P.M.s and who he had helped cut up. Some staff had said that he exaggerated and he certainly loved to wallow in a certain kind of importance which he thought assisting the pathologist deserved.

I had initially thought that his desire to work in a mortuary was unnatural and had tried to distance myself from him, especially when he made the tea on the ward. But today was different. He was my only source of reassurance and support and so I clung to him like a clam.

'Come closer,' Rob said. 'You won't see much from there.'

I had received plenty of advice from other members of the staff, on how to attend a P.M. 'Make sure you have something to eat,' was one source of advice.

'Never go on a full stomach, in case you are sick,' contradicted another.

'Take deep breaths, if you begin to think you will faint.'

'Eat mints, or something to take away the taste, and smell.'

'Look at the light, pretending you are looking at the body.'

'Think of something funny, or sexy, to take your mind off what is going on,' one nurse had said.

I liked that one, think of something funny in this situation! I was so nervous it nearly set me off with hysterical laughter.

I decided to look at the light when they began to make the incision. I was all right at the beginning, glancing at the body occasionally, but this strategy soon became flawed, as the pathologist started asking me questions, and

pointing out certain parts of the person's
anatomy. I was starting to feel sick and giddy
when the stomach contents were examined.
The pathologist pinched out a lump from
within the body and said it was an old T.B.
Nodule, holding it up under my nose.
Time for the deep breaths routine I thought as
my legs felt like jelly.
Suddenly Rob produced a saw and started
sawing away at the ribs.
This finished me. I took a few steps back.
'All right son?' asked the policeman. 'Go
outside for a breath of fresh air if you want.' I
said I was fine, even though I wasn't feeling
too good. I knew that it would be all around
the hospital if I left, or fainted, Rob would see
to that. The ribs were lifted away, exposing the
heart and lungs. They were cut out, examined
and weighed. The cause of death was
determined to be from a lung infection,
pneumonia and congestive heart failure.
Thank goodness for that I thought. It would
soon be over. I had nearly made it and began
to feel more confident and again edged
forward.
I stopped still in my tracks when I realised that

they were going to routinely examine the
brain. I really did feel sick, as they cut away
the top of the skull. I had seen a brain before,
in a tank of formaldehyde in the Path Lab, but
the thought of exposing one here, right in front
of me really did sicken me. My legs were
heavy and I began to fidget.
Suddenly there was a loud knock at the back
door and I nearly jumped out of my skin.
'See who that is,' Rob said.
I opened the door, gratefully breathing in the
surge of fresh air.
It was an undertaker, come to collect a body.
'I will give you a lift,' I volunteered, explaining
importantly that I was assisting with a P.M.
I assisted the undertaker to carry in the coffin.
We put the body into it and I made sure that
we took our time in tidying it up. We then
loaded the coffin into the hearse and I was
pleased when the undertaker offered me a
cigarette and wanted to chat.
On my return to the P.M. examination, I
explained what I had been doing and showed
mock disappointment when I saw the skull
was back in place, as I said I wanted to see the
brain.

I helped put the body back into the fridge and
was thanked for helping the undertaker.
I returned to my duties on the ward feeling
quite pleased with myself...and quietly
relieved.
When asked by another student, how it had
been, I replied: 'There was nothing to it,
haven't you been to one yet?'

The Hospital Chapel.

Sunday sevices were attended by patients and staff.
9-30am: Roman Catholic service.
11am: Church of England service.
2pm: Chapel service held by a Methodist Minister.
Patients were members of the choir.

Chapter eleven.

Charlie was told that he, and some of the other patients, were to see the ward doctor, and the charge nurse to discuss, their legal status under the Mental Health Act. He knew he was on a Section 26 as the Act had changed shortly after his admission to the hospital. At that time he had received a letter, from the hospital secretary, informing him of the change.

He had been told to open the letter and the nurse had taken it from him and filed it in his case notes. It stated he was on a section instead of being certified insane. The nurse said it meant that he still couldn't get out, but at least the hospital would have to review his case annually.

Charlie's turn came and he entered the charge nurses office where he was surprised to find Dr Minor whom he hadn't previously seen following his move to this ward.

'How are you Charlie?' enquired the doctor as he flicked through his notes.

'I've decided to change you to an informal patient as the managers are telling me that I have the highest number of detained patients in the hospital.'

'Thank-you, doctor,' Charlie muttered, not knowing what an informal patient was, he had been pre-warned by a sympathetic nurse to look grateful and say nothing.

Addressing the charge nurse, Dr Minor added: 'They say my figures look bad against the other doctors, and there is a team of inspectors, or someone coming to the hospital.'

'Well that's it,' he said to Charlie. 'You can go into the grounds but if you try to leave the hospital I will put you on a section again.'

'Who's next?' he asked the charge nurse as Charlie was summarily dismissed from his presence.

It was explained to Charlie that being an informal patient meant that he was there on his own free will, like the old voluntary patient. Charlie remembered Dr Minor's parting comment, but took heart in the knowledge that he would again be able to wander around the grounds of his own free will.

Today was picture day and he lined up in the corridor to be counted with the other patients who were going to the show. He might have been an informal patient but he did not feel anything was different in his circumstances. He liked to go to the pictures and was used to the routine.

They had all been spruced up, washed and shaved, and some of the patients had put on clean clothes. The staff, fearful of an outburst from the chief male nurse if any patient was seen with trousers halfway up their legs, tried to ensure that all garments fitted.

Unfortunately, some always seemed too short, no matter what the staff did, it was part of the patient's personality, like Paddy who wouldn't look right doing his jig if his trousers were a good fit. It just wouldn't have been him.

The hospital was making a big effort to personalise all patients' clothing, and a second tailor had been employed. He was known as 'Tom the Tailor' and was kept busy going around the wards, but he hadn't yet been to Charlie's ward to measure up. Each patient was to be provided with a suit, casual clothes, shirts and underwear.

'Twenty eight,' the nurse shouted back down to the ward and they all marched off. Well not so much march, Charlie thought, but at least they were walking with some purpose, even if it was only to the hall.

Up a long dark corridor they went, stopping to let another line of patients go by. At the top of the corridor it was already getting congested as everyone seemed to be arriving at the same time. Once in the hall, which could hold several hundred, they were directed to a row of seats...men on one side and women on the other.

Charlie watched as the other wards sorted out where everyone should sit. Some patients were moved next to a nurse whilst others were given sweets and cigarettes. Already some of the patients were turning around and begging for a 'fag' from those smoking behind them. Not all the patients were allowed to smoke as they didn't discard their stumps safely and there was only the already multiple cigarette burned wooden floor to put them out on.

Some burned their fingers, or their clothes which had been described as net   curtains by one cynic...because they had so many holes in them.

Eventually, everyone settled down and the lights dimmed though, occasionally a door would open and admit latecomers or members of staff who sneaked in to stand at the back of the hall.

Charlie felt as he did when he had been to the pictures in town. There seemed to be a feeling of expectancy, as if something exciting was going to happen when the lights went down. Even here he felt the same and he would soon be lost to the world on the screen. He loved the opening music and the cockerel doing its thing. The commentator took them through the news of the week, his voice rising and falling to meet the mood of his theme.

Then there was a short interval before the film began. It was never totally dark because the patients had to be observed, but it was dark enough to forget that the sun was out.

Today the film was about a sheep dog called 'Black Bob' and although it was colourful, Charlie soon lost interest and started looking around him.

All these people, he thought, sitting here as if they were just on an afternoon out.

The sight of all these patients in the hall reminded him of an old film he had seen about a mental hospital in America, It had been called 'The Snake Pit,' and had starred one of

his favourite actresses Olivia de Havilland
who played a lady who had fallen in love
before becoming mentally ill. Some of the
scenes were not unlike those he had witnessed
here with the frightening bit about E.C.T. He
also remembered about the patients' dances
where they all picked their partners. The best
part was when she got out of hospital and, he
hoped, lived happily ever afterwards.
Charlie was jerked out of his reverie by a
nearby patient who jumped up, saluted, and
shouted 'God save the Queen'.
Not him again he thought as his heart returned
to something close to its normal beat.
'You soft bastard,' he muttered. 'You could
have given me a heart attack; they should give
you some E.C.T.'
He looked at the screen to see the sheep dog
going for help after his owner had injured his
leg in a fall. The music played faster to give
more suspense and atmosphere and some of
the patients were shouting encouragement to
Black Bob.
Charlie was at his most cynical after being
startled by the 'Queen's guard'.
'It's only a film, you stupid idiots,' he shouted.

'He can't hear you.'
'But I can hear you, Charlie,' a nurse said from the gloom. 'You'll be back on the ward if you don't keep quiet.'
Charlie said nothing else that afternoon and sulked as they stood up to sing the national anthem. The 'guard' stood rigid, with his arm stiff to his head, in salute, singing at the top of his voice.
'You'll stick like that if the wind changes,' he muttered under his breath, remembering the phrase his granny had often used when she found him sulking over something he couldn't have. He had seen patients on the ward stuck in unusual positions, never moving or speaking.

*****

Some of the most bizarre set of symptoms I had ever seen were demonstrated by a Jewish patient named Isaac. He was suffering from Catatonic Schizophrenia and had long periods of what seemed to me fairly normal behaviour, but then, occasionally, and quite alarmingly he slipped into a catatonic stupor.

When this happened he would lie in his bed and would not move unless a member of staff attended to him. They would change his position, or get him up. Even when he was sitting up in a chair he would not move and became incontinent. He only ate or drank when the staff fed him and when he was in a deep stupor it was necessary to tube feed him. The nurse in charge told me he portrayed symptoms of what was known as 'waxy flexibility'. He stood Isaac up from his chair and took him to the middle of the room where he pulled out his right arm, side ways, and then bent his left arm as if he was flexing his biceps. A quarter of an hour later Isaac remained in precisely the same position and stayed there until he was put to sit down.

He did not speak, but as he was beginning to come out of it, he started to repeat things that were said to him. It was a feature of his illness and was known as 'echolalia'.

'Come to the toilet Isaac,' said a nurse who got an instant reply, 'Come to the toilet Isaac'!

A fellow patient shouted: 'Shut up you silly man,' only to have it immediately repeated, 'Shut up you silly man.'

This was often hilarious, but on other occasions it could be very frustrating, especially when you were trying to get him to respond to your requests.

Some patients suffering from a catatonic illness would also copy movements carried out by others, though I never saw Isaac do it. This was known as 'echopraxia'.

Although he did not speak for nearly two weeks I was amazed to find that he said he could remember all that had gone on when he was in his stupor. In fact, he reported some members of staff to the doctor for taking the 'mickey' out of him. A misinterpretation of events, or delusions, was generally sufficient to get the staff off the hook.

The most alarming thing to me was that when Isaac did finally surface from his catatonic state he became very excitable, running around the ward and becoming aggressive and troublesome to all those around him.

His treatment was very hard to prescribe. He had been having E.C.T. when he was low, but now he needed tranquillising to calm him down. It was extremely difficult for medical and nursing staff to modify his mood, as he

see-sawed from one extreme to the other.
When he was low and having E.C.T. twice a
week, the staff had the problems of getting him
up and down the stairs, as the treatment was
given on another ward which was on the other
side of the hospital. Isaac would not move
from one step to another and we had to
practically move each leg for him. In the end it
became much easier to carry him down.
One of the most important lessons I learned
about this, and other mental illnesses, was not
to take at face value what you saw, or thought
what might happen. A patient who was in a
catatonic stupor for a long time could suddenly
jump out of bed and perhaps attack you. This
was quite frightening at first and it made me
wary when I was alone with Isaac. I would
look into his vacant face and wonder what was
going on in his head and what he would do
next. But after days of silence and inactivity,
my guard would drop and I would relax, only
to nearly jump out of my skin when he
suddenly dived out of his chair and charged
across the room.
Sometimes you could be sitting there day
dreaming and you might also be attacked by a

patient who was hallucinating, listening to, and obeying the 'voices'. I soon found out who was prone to this behaviour, but it was usually the exception rather than the rule to be attacked. Often it could be attributed to inexperience or the mishandling of a situation by the nurse, or provocation by another patient. Even so, the old hands always warned you to sit or stand with your back against the wall.

Chapter twelve.

I had not been on the wards very long before I was approached by the secretary of one of the trade unions in the hospital C.O.H.S.E. (Confederation of Health Service Employees). He said it was in my own interest to join the union which would give me some form of protection if anything went wrong. I asked him what he meant and he told me that the union was always fighting for better working conditions for staff, such as higher wages, a shorter working week, and more holidays. He also said he would represent me if I got into a situation involving disciplinary action. I couldn't imagine myself being involved in anything like that, but he told me of cases of persistent sickness, lateness, or errors in the treatment of patients by staff.

There were three main organisations in the hospital that represented the staff; N.U.P.E. (National Union of Public Employees), which he said was mainly for the ancillary staff; C.O.H.S.E., the union for the majority of the mental nurses; and the R.C.N. (The Royal College of Nursing) which was not recognised as a trade union but whose members were mostly general nurses. I commented that I really liked the idea of joining the R.C.N. as they sounded the most professional. He went mad and said I would not be accepted by the 'rest' and to keep well away from them. In the end I relented and joined C.O.H.S.E. with an instruction to pay my subscriptions each week to the treasurer who could be found standing near the pay queue.

The staff salaries were paid out in the main hall at lunchtime each Thursday. There were two pay points, one for the male nursing staff, and one for the ancillary and building staff. A senior nurse sat next to a member of staff from the wages department and ticked off our name from a long list, before the wages were handed over.

My weekly wages, since I started on the wards, had doubled from £3.00 to nearly £6.00, so I enthusiastically handed over my first contribution of sixpence to the union treasurer.

I quickly became an active member of the union, attended all the branch meetings and was elected to the executive committee soon after I had joined. In spite of my enthusiasm, I soon realised that unless there was something major happening in the hospital that affected the staff, not many people attended meetings. I was still interested in the framework and history of the health service, especially mental illness, and was eager to study the role the unions played. I learned that two unions had amalgamated to form C.O.H.S.E. in 1946. The Mental hospital and Institution Workers Union grew out of a union formed for asylum workers in 1910. The Hospital and Welfare Services Union had its roots in a union formed for poor law workers after the First World War. From my studies I found that the people confined to the asylums lived in an environment that was often no more than being barely adequate for human habitation. It also meant, of course, that the people employed to look after them had to endure the same conditions. Patients living in cramped and crowded wards meant the staff had to work in the same environment and, on top of this, they had to work with basic equipment and were often subjected to hostilities and unprovoked attacks. Asylum staff were also vulnerable to contracting infectious diseases, such as tuberculosis and typhoid fever.

Not surprisingly, there was a shortage of suitable people who wished to become nurses or attendants. Staffing had been altogether inadequate during the wars and a terrible burden had been placed on existing staff. In addition, successive governments had continued to fail those who worked in the health service. I could see that the unions had a major role to play in fighting for a satisfactory living wage and a reduction in the long working hours. This spurred me on to be a good steward and trade union member.

But my efforts were frustrated, time and time again. The apathy and selfishness of some of the staff was unbelievable. There seemed to be an 'as long as I am all right Jack' culture in the hospital and it was an effort to get members to attend meetings, or support union action, which weakened our cause. Yet when they had a problem of their own, we were expected to stop everything and immediately be at their beck and call. The only time they stood together was over pay and hours of duty.

Some of the older staff who had worked at the

hospital for forty years told me that the staff
never used to have proper accommodation and
would sleep on the wards, in order to be
'available' for emergencies and disturbances.
Even their meals had to be eaten on the wards
in the old asylums...and the food was part of
their wages!

Discipline was harsh. Asylums were run on
strict disciplinarian lines. The male staff had
the appearance of warders, dressed in dark
uniforms and wore peaked caps. The head of
the asylum was the medical superintendent and
his word was law. Each asylum was inspected
by a visiting committee who issued books of
staff rules which even included, in one case,
how much water should be used in a bath, i.e.
the permitted depth, in inches, but most of the
rules related to security and it was often instant
dismissal if they were disobeyed or neglected.

In the Committee of Visitors report 1854
conditions in the Chester asylum were
compared with the other local asylums,
Rainhill and Prestwich. The staffing at Chester
was much lower than both.

The staffing problem still existed a century
later, despite the fact that the union had

regularly demonstrated to management what
the staffing establishment should be for each
ward. Even when the staffing numbers were
higher, the skill mix was invariably low. A
third year student nurse was often expected to
take charge of a ward at night and sometimes
on the less demanding wards, during the day.
The female wards were desperately
short of qualified and full time nursing staff.

*****

Charlie always hated bath day, not that he
didn't want the pleasures of a nice long hot
bath, he longed for one, but here it was more
like a sheep dip.
As extra staff were required, bath day was
designated to the same day each week for each
ward, which also ensured the water remained
hot and was not being used in large quantities
by any of the adjacent wards.
On Charlie's ward, bath day was always
Wednesday.
All the patients were kept in the ward after
breakfast and some remained in their night
clothes. Extra laundry was delivered, including

several extra bags of towels.

Charlie always tried to get near the front of the queue. Mainly to get his bath over with, but also to get a pick of the clean socks, underwear and shirts that were piled up in the bathroom, in neat stacks. It gave him the chance to get something that would nearly fit him, as it was always pot-luck, especially for those at the rear of the queue.

A skip for the dirty clothes stood nearby, for everything except the socks which went into a separate bag. The socks were grey and had a red ring around their top.

Nurses, usually according to their seniority, were allocated to the different tasks of bathing the patients. The senior nurse supervised the whole operation and kept a bath book up to date. This entailed recording each bath, whether nails had been cut, and documenting any marks, or bruising, that had been observed.

The bathroom was situated in the sanitary annexe area of the ward, adjacent to the wash-room and toilets, and was usually cold during the winter. Because of this windows could not be opened, adding to the damp, steamy atmosphere.

Charlie would leave most of his belongings in his locker, as he knew from experience that a lot of pilfering went on, especially when you were left standing naked and helpless or, worse, you were in the bath.

There were three baths on this ward, and a nurse was allocated to each one. The tap heads were removable, as they had been in Charlie's previous ward, these were operated by a nurse. The water was emptied from the bath by a foot pedal on the outside of the bath.

Charlie joined the queue of half naked bodies and was told to strip off the remainder of his clothes which were thrown into the skip.

There were six patients in front of him and, soon, as many behind him. They all stood in a line waiting for a vacant bath, each aware of the others body odour. Dignity, as Charlie had discovered long ago, was non existent. Some covered their genitals with their hands whilst others just stood there, not appearing to bother whether they were dressed or not. He hated it when someone pushed from the back so their bodies came into contact in a degrading sense of intimacy.

The baths filled and emptied with a consistent regularity and Charlie had learned that speed was the essence if you wanted to get a proper bath.

His turn soon came and fresh water was soon pouring into an empty bath. The nurse checked the temperature of the water with a bath thermometer and Charlie was told to get in. At least, being near to the front, he was given a large piece of soap which came in bars which were cut down from blocks of about eighteen inches.

Already aware of the nurse telling him to hurry up, he quickly soaped the lower part of his body, but before he had hardly started to wash himself, shampoo was poured over his head. 'Rub that in,' he was told and before he had finished a bowl of water was poured over him. Charlie splashed and spluttered, rubbed the soap out of his eyes and tried to complete his bath as the nurse started to let out the water.

Up and out within minutes and the bath was already being filled for the next patient. Charlie moved into the wash-room and grabbed a towel.

'Let's see your nails,' another nurse said, so

Charlie obediently put his foot on a towel placed over the nurse's knee and his toe nails were cut.

'Hands!' He stretched out his hands and his fingernails were cut.

Shivering with cold, Charlie threw his damp towel into the skip, grabbed some clean clothes and hurriedly got dressed. He cleared the steam from the mirror, to comb his hair and watched his reflection disappear in the condensation.

He was thankful that another bath day was over.

Sitting in the day-room afterwards enjoying a cigarette he watched a nurse chase up the stragglers who were reluctant to go for their bath. They were like naughty children, Charlie thought. Some wouldn't get undressed, others refused to change their clothes and some didn't know they were supposed to have a bath.

Charlie remembered when he was a child that they always had a 'bath day' in his house. So did all the neighbours, as they shared a washhouse, and heated the water with a fire beneath the boiler. His bath day was usually on a late Saturday afternoon, so that they would be clean to go to church the next day.

They had used an old tin bath that hung, from a big nail in the wall outside the house. It was freezing in the winter and sometimes, when they were very small, they were bathed in the sink, in the washhouse across the yard. The tin bath was brought into the house and placed on the kitchen floor with old newspapers under it to stop the 'lino' getting wet. The hot water was carried to the house in buckets, drawn from the boiler in the washhouse.

Charlie thought of how many of them had needed to use that water, especially if his mother had gone first. It made him think twice about criticising the staff here.

He had seen one of them make some of the patients use the same water to save time. At least those at home had been family. He smiled at the way he taunted his sisters by saying he had 'peed' in the water...

The sound of the tea arriving snapped him out of his reverie and he waited for the ward to be opened up again so he could return to his corner in the 'backs.'

The staff restaurant.
Breakfast, dinner, tea and supper was served
during the day, and an evening meal was
provided up to 2am for the night staff.
The day time services were attended by
waiters who came from Spain and Italy.

Chapter Thirteen.

Nurses were encouraged, and were eager, to organise activities for the patients out in the community. Trips to the seaside, especially Blackpool and the illuminations were always popular as was the annual ward trip with a stop for fish and chips on the way back. On weekends some of the patients also enjoyed the short coach trip to watch the staff football team when they were playing away in the local league.

Holidays were also being considered for those patients who could appreciate them, and some staff and patients went away for weekends. There had also been an exchange visit with patients from a hospital in South Wales although this had been criticised by some as going from one asylum to another but then, the proposed holiday destinations were becoming more ambitious.

I am a keen football fan and always go to watch Liverpool's home games. I am also an agent for the club and so was very enthusiastic when, with two of my colleagues, we decided to organise a trip to Anfield. I wrote to the club outlining our proposal to take some of the patients to watch a match and we were delighted to be issued with ten free tickets for an evening game in the European cup against Reykjavik, an Icelandic side. It was agreed by the senior staff at the hospital that three staff and seven patients would attend and we were to travel in the smaller of the two hospital buses.

We selected Derek who lived and breathed Liverpool F.C., a patient who spent hours embroidering pictures that had been drawn for him, always with the theme of LFC...His locker was always stuffed up with comics, pictures and football books, all to do with Liverpool. Derek was a bit slow on the uptake and, at times, could be very stubborn. He did not know when enough was enough and, unfortunately for him, he did tend to annoy people which did not help in his relationships. He was also an epileptic and could become aggressive and so needed skilful handling. J.C., was a favourite of mine and my colleagues, was also chosen...if he wasn't too 'high'. J.C. was an extremely energetic person and, if he was in a hypo-manic state, he would dress in loud and colourful clothes. He usually had some gadget with him, a radio full on, some unusual kind of toy, or flowers and badges, and even flashing lights on his clothes. You normally heard him before you saw him! He was also a capable artiste who could play the guitar, and often sang his own composed songs.

The third patient would be Franco who loved football. He was middle-aged but still played in goal for the patients' side and at cricket he could bowl an acceptable googly. Franco's problem was that he believed he was the King of Spain and often wrote to the Spanish Embassy, telling them so. He was extremely paranoid and claimed he could see what he called our 'spiritual guides'. These 'guides' told him whether you were a good or an evil person and this he would express publicly about different members of staff. Fortunately he said that my 'guide' was a good one.

Ivy was a middle aged lady who was free to wander around the hospital doing whatever she pleased. She was supposed to be running errands for the ward, but spent most of her time in the canteen drinking tea and smoking.

She accompanied the men to watch the football, cricket, anything that was going on, and although she was not thought to be interested in football we asked her because she loved trips. She was content as long as she had her packet of fags and people left her alone. If they didn't she was more than capable of winning an argument with anybody. She was diagnosed as a schizophrenic.

The other three patients, Harry, Bill and George, were seasoned travellers on most trips from the hospital and they loved nothing better than to stop for a pint on the way back. They had been to Anfield before, but not officially. I had once taken them to queue with me for derby tickets, the allocation being one per person, and my mates could not get off work. I had taken them over to Liverpool, given them the money for the tickets, and put them in front of me in the queue; we waited an hour but they coped well. On the way back to the hospital we stopped for fish and chips and then I bought them a pint, adding the cost to the tickets. I had said that I was integrating them within the community, and they appeared to have enjoyed themselves.

On the day of the match, it was September, we all met in the hospital reception at 5.45pm. I had recently got engaged to the nurse I was courting and she came too see us off. She was concerned there might be a danger of fog, especially around the Merseyside area, but cheered up when she saw our 'supporters'.

With me were two other nurses, Mick, who checked that all the patients had pocket money, and Jim who was the driver.

Derek was over-dressed in all his Liverpool gear...scarf, hat, badges and a home made flag. I thought how conspicuous he would look at the match and that was something we didn't really want.

J.C. was singing, when he wasn't winding Derek up and Ivy, who sat at the back of the bus, soon had a blue cloud forming around her as she began to chain smoke. Franco was heard to ask her where we were going to be in Liverpool, and we were on our guard in case he tried to do a 'runner'.

Jim was not used to driving the bus, but he landed us safely in a side street near the ground.

'Mind your car?' asked a lad who looked no

older than eight years old.

'It'll be more for a bus,' he said, 'It's taking up all my space. I'll see that nobody robs it,' he assured us as he climbed on to the bumper.

'O.K.,' I said, and told him that we would pay him when we returned, I was used to the patter and knew he would disappear if we gave him the money in advance.

We were soon mingling with the football crowd, but as we waited for Derek to return from the toilet, J.C. suddenly shot off. He had spotted a camera crew and by the time we reacted he had interrupted a T.V. reporter and had stuck his head in front of the camera, talking to it in his usual maniacal way.

'Hello, I'm J.C. a famous disc jockey and your going to get stuffed tonight, by Liverpool, the best team in the world.'

He ended up giving an interview but fortunately for all concerned it was for Iceland T.V., though this did not bother J.C.

The tickets were for the Kemlyn Road stand, and we had good seats, opposite the half way line. The ground wasn't full as it was only a preliminary round match and Liverpool had won the away leg 5-0.

Nevertheless we were still excited and it was a totally new experience for the patients, though Jim had watched Chester. My colleague Mike was an Evertonian, but he certainly wasn't saying so.

J.C. enjoyed singing with the kop but the others looked bewildered, except for Derek who was already attracting unwanted attention from the row behind with his enthusiastic flag waving, narrowly missing a Scouser's right eye, with his elbow.

'Watch what your doing with that flag,' said the startled Scouser.

'What's the matter with you?' drooled Derek, turning round to look at him.

'Watch where you stick your elbow,' replied the annoyed Scouser.

'I'm only waving my flag; what's the matter with you mate?' repeated Derek. 'Where's Billy Liddell?'

'Billy Liddell? Where's he been?' responded the Scouser, to nobody in particular, but to anybody who was listening.

'The lunatic asylum,' chipped in J.C. sarcastically.

'That's where he should be,' came the reply

from behind, followed by laughter, and this set off the tone for the rest of the match.

'Sit down, all of you,' I cried, with embarrassment, glad that the teams had come out. I tried to placate the occupants of the row behind us with small talk and body gestures, hoping they would appreciate our plight.

As soon as they kicked off, Ivy wanted the toilet and as she was sitting in the middle, we all had to stand to let her out. This was repeated on several occasions during the match.

The crowd at least became friendlier as Liverpool scored two goals.

Franco followed Ivy to the toilets and Derek was still asking about Billy Liddel, much to the amusement of some of the spectators, though he was starting to irritate the guy in front of him which was not helped by J.C.'s mocking and running commentary of the match.

'Who wants tea?' Mick asked at half-time as Jim and I stayed with the patients. We didn't take much notice of a commotion in the area near the ladies' toilets.

Mick was pushed and shoved, but eventually

got two drinks, the only amount he could manage to carry, with so much pushing.

Ivy wasn't in sight, so we started to pay attention to the noise coming from the toilet area and I went to see what was happening. There was a long queue...women were wriggling, trying to stand with their legs crossed, some were red faced and others were banging on the toilet door. I was about to move away when I heard the distinct cry of Ivy shouting obscenities from the other side of the door.

'F*** off,' she was screaming in her best fishwife voice. I was afraid of what she'd do if someone got hold of her as her looks were deceptive and she was capable of sorting them all out.

She had barricaded herself into the toilet to continue her chain-smoking and wasn't going to come out and sit in the 'bloody' cold for anyone. The situation was resolved with the help of the stewards and after much abuse we returned to our seats.

The game was very one-sided and Liverpool scored six goals. It became like a practice match and did not hold the crowd's attention who were now cheering the opposition and booing Liverpool for fun.

Those close by started to focus their attentions on Derek again.

'Where's Billy Liddell?' droned Derek again, waving his arms about.

'Shut up, and put your arms down,' said the now angry Scouser from behind who was rapidly gaining support from those around him.

'What's wrong with you mate?' retorted Derek, standing up.

'Sit down and put that flag down before I stick it up your a***.'

'Don't speak to him like that,' interrupted J.C. On the advice of the steward we left early, much to the laughter of the crowd who had finally realised where we came from. The only one not laughing was the guy in front who caught dribble on his head as Derek protested.

'Where are we going? It's not finished yet and where's Billy Liddell?'

We hurried down the steps and went to the toilet; we soon became aware that we were one short, Franco.

I blamed Mike and Mike blamed Jim, but in

truth no-one had seen him go. We had just presumed that he had followed us into the toilet but, being the master of escape, he had probably gone off to claim his Spanish crown. As he had done it before we could, at least, guess what he would be trying to do and in the past he was brought back to the hospital by the police. It was just embarrassment of losing him after we had been warned he might run off.

*****

There were times when social functions could not be held in the main hall, i.e. when patients' beds occupied it whilst a ward was undergoing major renovations. Sometimes there would be up to sixty beds tightly packed in the hall and cadet nurses would be delegated to make them up each morning. They always complained that it took too long and caused them to miss their P.T sessions. In fact, everyone seemed bad tempered when patients were sleeping in the hall. The hall stank, as many of the beds were wet and dirty. Some of the patients' belongings, kept in bundles under the beds, were frequently mixed up or lost, adding to general bad feeling.

One day Charlie was told that he and the other patients would have to sleep in the main hall each night as their ward was to be upgraded. During the day they were split up and sent to stay on other wards where they were given their meals and, at 7-30 each night, sent to the main hall to sleep.

On the day of the changes there was an air of chaos and disruption as over sixty beds were taken apart and carried on trolleys to the main hall. Everyone seemed to be there, from the highest to the lowest. There were bosses directing the chaos and causing greater confusion; there was the porter and some of the workmen putting the beds back together; the gardeners helping to move the beds and extra nursing staff, assisted by the aggrieved cadets, making them up again. In addition some of the able-bodied patients were fetching and carrying as required. Charlie helped to bring up some of the bedding.

The beds were arranged in four rows and one chief wanted them facing this way, whist the charge nurse wanted them facing the other way. Tempers were short and the charge nurse won the argument, but it did not do much for his long term relationship with the chief when he shouted, 'Who's ward is it anyway?'

That evening Charlie and the rest of the patients were marched up the corridor and lined up outside the main hall. The charge nurse had remained on duty with one of the chief male nurses to manage the operation. Each patient in the queue was handed a nightshirt and directed to an appropriate bed...the trouble was, some of the patients wanted to go to the toilet and when they returned rejoined the queue. Some were therefore allocated two beds and very soon there appeared to be a shortage.

Charlie was allocated a bed near the top end of the hall and was dismayed by the chaos that ensued. He wished he had been given a place at the end of the row. He got undressed, folded his clothes, the best way he could, and placed his valuables in his pillowcase. He got into bed and surveyed what reminded him of a scene from a school history book depicting the horrors of the Crimean war. There was a mass of patients' heads sticking up as they sat bewildered by their new environment. Some did not seem able to comprehend that they were not here for the pictures and stared vacantly at the stage as if waiting for something to happen. The staff quickly lost their tempers and muttered obscenities under their breath about the management who, according to them, 'couldn't organise a p*** up in a brewery'!

Eventually the lights went out, but Charlie did not feel tired and doubted if he could sleep anyway.

The hall was impressive with wood panelled walls and magnificent ceiling beams, but there was also an air duct, near to Charlie's bed which at first was a blessing but later turned into a nightmare as the feral cats started courting. Their cries even frightened the night staff at first.

When he had been a boy, Charlie had stayed in the country with his grannie when she was visiting one of her daughters. He remembered the first night he had stayed in the room on his own. It had been pitch black and the depth of the darkness and the countryside noises had terrified him. He remembered he had singed a bed sheet when he had tried to light a candle; he also remembered the warm kind of feeling in his chest as he watched the flickering candle. It had brought tears to his eyes as he imagined the flame as a dancing fairy, he wished he could regain the good times he had had with his granny.

In the main hall, the second night was more chaotic than the first, nobody could find their original beds, and as Charlie lay there he concentrated on the stage area, noting the thick drape curtains, the coat of arms and motifs and the painted over windows, presumably to keep the light out, otherwise you would not see the films clearly. He drifted off to sleep picturing in his mind a scene from the film, 'The fall of the House of Usher'.

Hospital Fire Brigade 1905

The hospital provided a volunteer
fire service. During the war staff were on fire
watch during the night in case of air raids.

Chapter Fourteen.

The next ward to which I was allocated was
the one that looked after the epileptic patients.
It was called Male 5 and it had over 40 beds. I
had not looked forward to working here
because the charge nurse had a reputation   for
being very strict, and also because of the
nature of the patients who were mainly
psychotic as well as suffering from a severe
form of epilepsy. As was common with other
hospitals in the region all these patients were
nursed together in the same ward, whereas in
other parts of the country some epileptics were
nursed in separate hospitals, referred to as
'colonies'.
I started on M.5 on the afternoon shift and as I
climbed the stone steps that led up to the ward,
I felt there was a definite atmosphere, of
tension, although admittedly some of this was
certainly self-induced as I was nervous. It was
as if the whole place was about to explode and,
as I was to find out later, it often did,
especially when the charge nurse was off.
I entered the day-room and there was the
perpetual cloud of smoke hanging in the air.

The patients just seemed to stare at me as I reported for duty at the office. I had been pre-warned that they were always suspicious of new staff and they usually took their time in accepting you, if they ever accepted you at all. I was informed that all the patients had unintentionally formed themselves into different groups, of about six or seven, and that they sat together, had their meals together and 'looked out' for each other. It was the rivalry between these groups that caused a lot of the atmosphere on the ward, as petty quarrels would often flare up, sometimes leading to fights. Each group had its own leader, usually the strongest personality amongst them, and they also held some kind of rank within the ward, such as kitchen man or ward messenger. This 'leader' also gained favour with the staff because they could control the actions of 'their group'.

I soon discovered that a new member of staff was often reliant on winning the respect of some of these patients, before they could be accepted on the ward. I was also told that the fights could sometimes be quite vicious and so I was shown the acceptable methods of restraint and how patients should be put into the padded cell where they could be held until their behaviour modified, which could mean anything from hours to several days.

Sometimes they were brought out prematurely, if a more urgent case arose involving another patient who needed to be 'boxed up'.

There was also, apparently, an unwritten code of conduct on the ward which meant no matter how much patients hated each other they never took advantage if someone was experiencing a fit.

Epilepsy has been described by various historians since biblical times. It was sometimes described as 'sleeping sickness'. For centuries such seizures were thought to be due to the person being possessed by evil spirits and the superstitious feared them.

There were several types of epilepsy identified on the ward and I had been taught about some of them at the training school. There were the generalised convulsions, with involuntary movements of the whole body, and loss of consciousness. This was called Grand Mal epilepsy and was the common type on the ward. There were focal fits which could be either motor or sensory and did not progress to loss of consciousness. Motor fits could progressively involve the limbs and face on one side of the body known as 'Jacksonian fits'. Sensory fits are experienced similarly as a travelling sensation involving a limb or part of the body. Minor fits, or petit mal, were simple brief losses of consciousness without movement.

The anti convulsant medication was mainly Epanutin and Phenobarbitone.

I was also told that although the patients received this medication, fits were still frequent and that occasionally someone would have a series of fits which could not be controlled easily and were sometimes life threatening. This was known as Status Epilepticus.

The main part of the ward was the day-room and its central piece of furniture (common in most male wards) was a full sized snooker table with eight beautifully carved wooden legs. There was the traditional hooded light above, and the scoreboard with brass markers. The cues were kept locked up in the office as they could become dangerous weapons in the wrong hands. Apart from the weekends, the staff or patients were not allowed to play snooker until after tea. The table was kept covered with a large cloth and was brushed and ironed religiously most days.

The armchairs, heavy to prevent the patients from throwing them, were arranged around the perimeter of the room. The dining area was made up of tables and chairs which were situated near to the kitchen.

I also realised there were two important doors to take note of in the day-room, one led to the charge nurse's office, the other to the pads'. There were times when both staff and patients watched both doors apprehensively.

The next lesson I learnt was that there were strict rules in place to prevent patients from harming themselves or committing aggressive acts when fits occurred. Drinking tumblers were plastic and cutlery was counted every night and kept in a locked box; the patients with homicidal tendencies were only allowed to use plastic crockery and I was warned to watch that they did not try to take or hide other patients' knives and forks. The fireguards were always kept locked and only designated patients were allowed to open them to put coal on to the fire.

As was standard practice with all wards, the bath had removable tap keys and the lavatories were operated by pedals rather than chains.

On this ward, and its female equivalent, the beds were only inches from the floor, again to prevent the patient from harm if he fell out during a fit. It was a back breaking task making them each day.

The dormitory had three tightly packed rows of low beds, each with a hard pillow and a rubber chamber pot. Every morning a patient, Edgar, collected the pots and piled them, one on top of the other, before emptying their contents down the sluice. He looked like someone from Covent Garden as he carried them out, ten high, and sometimes he would spill them.

The bottom of the dormitory had a row of side rooms with glass slits in their doors to enable the staff to observe the occupants. Each room window was covered with a wooden shutter, as these housed the more severe cases on the ward. The patients were locked up at night as there was only one night nurse in attendance.

He would have to contact the duty charge nurse if a patient became disturbed or agitated and he would not enter the room on his own. My initial apprehension about working on this ward soon disappeared once I had a few days' experience. I soon got to know the patients and started to read some of their case notes. Some had been here for most of their adult lives and their ages ranged from eighteen to eighty. This surprised me, but the older ones could often be as agile as the youngsters when aggressive and certainly couldn't have been looked after with the geriatric patients.

There were many characters amongst these patients. Some were amusing in their behaviour and actions, while others were unpredictable. They could be extremely violent, mostly towards each other, but sometimes towards the staff. There were those aggressive by nature, known as psychopaths. Then there were those who only became dangerous after a fit. They had no control or insight into their behaviour and were generally placid in nature the rest of the time.

There were also patients who were child like, with below average intelligence and who didn't know their own strength. When they had tantrums they could throw a dining chair at someone, or slap a nurse across the face, as perhaps would a toddler. The only difference being that a toddler was twenty pounds but these patients were nearly twenty stone and could nearly knock you out.

I was warned that one patient in particular, Ray, was extremely dangerous, especially before and after a fit, and required skilled handling. Ray had a history of breaking a nurses arm, but most of the time he displayed child-like behaviour and responded to being humoured. He was one patient who was given extra helpings of rice pudding.

Experienced nurses on the ward could anticipate when the majority of fits were going to occur. This was especially so in Grand Mal epilepsy which had three stages, sometimes four.

The first stage was the Aura. This was something that the patient experienced, or felt, and acted as a warning. Not all patients experienced this, but those who did sometimes had to sit, or lie down, away from harm. Some had feelings of unreality; some had smells, like smelling gas, and several became dizzy, or anxious.

The second stage was the Tonic stage when the patient lost consciousness. Some cried out loudly as they fell or sometimes crashed to the ground, with all their muscles in spasm. Their breathing would stop and they often became cyanosed. Often their backs were curved and their faces contorted. This stage lasted about thirty seconds. Because of the severity and frequency of their fits some patients wore padded head guards as they had previously experienced serious head wounds.

The third stage was the Clonic stage when there were regular jerky movements, breathing resumed, and the tongue was often bitten, to try and prevent this mouth gags were strategically placed around the ward. Sometimes a patient would be incontinent. Afterwards a deep sleep would usually follow. Some patients came around quickly, often confused, and with a headache. Others felt refreshed and released from their tensions.

The part of the sequence I had not seen, or heard of previously was called the Fugue. Instead of returning to their normal state, the behaviour of some patients changed. Some were violent and were often moved to a place of safety before they recovered, another would always attempt to go to the kitchen for a knife. The strangest behaviour I saw on the ward was a patient running around the day-room on all fours and barking like a dog. He actually chased the staff and tried to bite their legs. Eventually I found it funny, but at first it was quite frightening to have a bald headed, middle-aged man, running around on all fours, barking and trying to snap at your legs. The first time it happened I jumped on the snooker table in fright, only for the patient to jump up after me.

After the first month, I had become quite an expert in dealing with these patients and the daily routine was pretty much the same as on a long-stay ward. The last patients to be attended to each morning were the ones sleeping in the side rooms, or anyone in the pads. You always went into the pads in pairs, or with more staff if necessary, until the occupant's behaviour had been assessed.

Patients on the ward were occupied with manual work, especially in the mornings when the ward was cleaned, and six were allowed to work outside; as well as a small group on a barrow gang cleaning up the grounds.

The main emphasis was always on security and safety, and this was how the work was allocated No sharp tools, no heights to climb, and no access to fires or electricity. The more dependent patients were left to sit by the fire or a window. The emphasis with these patients was comfort rather then rehabilitation.

Church groups visited the ward and sang to the patients, and once a week they played Lotto for sweets and cigarettes. Those able were escorted to the weekly dance or picture show. Most of the ward activity revolved around the snooker table, watching or playing. Some of the patients were excellent snooker players having played daily for most of their time on the ward. At the end of my placement on this ward I was surprised how my attitude had changed, I really had liked working there although I was still wary of some of the patients behaviour. Others felt the same, and when they visited the shop they often jumped the queue by mutual consent from the other patients in the hospital.

*****

Charlie woke up and looked about him. They were back in their newly decorated ward and clean curtains covered the windows. It seemed brighter now and not only was it due to the new paint on the walls, the light shades had been washed to remove the hundreds of insect corpses that Charlie had gazed at each night. For once his mind seemed clear and he was able to contemplate his surroundings in a more logical way. He didn't often have these clear heads...more, as he called it, a 'woolly' headed feeling of not being quite aware of where he was.

'What am I doing here?' he asked himself, not for the first time since his admission. He closed his eyes and pulled the sheet over his head and started thinking about his childhood. This always made him feel more secure, even if sometimes the memories were painful. His mind slowly drifted to church and he started to hear the old songs and hymns he used to sing. He saw the vicar standing in front of the small congregation singing, 'What a friend we have in Jesus, all our sins and griefs to bear.' The tears had flowed down his cheeks as he had gone forward to make his testimony and stand next to the vicar who welcomed him with open arms. Once a month someone would get up and open their hearts to the congregation, confessing their sins and telling how Jesus Christ had saved them. A reformed alcoholic said he had crawled out of the gutter into the arms of Jesus and had become the Church's 'holy warrior,' fighting against the perils of the demon drink. Charlie seemed to remember all he had said and how he had faced the people who seemed to condemn him, for even though they had smiles on their faces, their eyes were hostile. They knew he was mad.

'Do you know what it is like to be mad?' he asked them.

'I mean, thought to be mad, when you see yourself as being normal?'

Slowly the church of his childhood drifted away and he saw the church in the hospital full of nurses.

He addressed them with a new vengeance in his voice.

'I know 'normal' people who are mad,' he said.

'Some of you nurses are mad. Some of you nurses are actually psychotic, no insight, no depth of feeling. You have no feelings about what you inflict on your fellow man, and you actually believe you are caring for us', he shouted, now thumping his fist into his other hand. 'It's sad to think that man is capable of looking at his own 'brother' and not seeing himself in him, or even recognise his own species. And sadder still, you become man's biggest tormentors.'

He paused, and his voice was a whisper when he continued, just like the vicar had told his stories.

'I went to a staff members funeral once. I didn't want to go, but you said it would look good for the family and his colleagues if patient's attended. They said he would go to heaven, after devoting his life to caring for others. He probably thought that too; forgetting the pain, the humiliation, the bullying, he had inflicted on us.'

'It's very easy to get into this habit of making evil appear good, but you'll say I'm paranoid, so you will always be right, and I will always be wrong.'

One of the nurses smiled and said, 'Sit down Charlie, you're not well.'

'It's fate, Charlie cried.' 'You get the white coat and I get the straight Jacket, you have the needle and I'm in the pads.'

They were answering him now. 'Come on Charlie, get that sheet off your face and get up,' the nurse said, bringing him back to reality with a start.

He removed the sheet from his flushed and sweating face.

'What's up Charlie, caught you masturbating have I?' he joked.

In his head Charlie was still preaching the gospel of human rights and couldn't separate fantasy from reality.

'Don't speak to me like that,' he screamed at the nurse.

'O.K. Charlie, quieten down I was only joking,' the nurse replied, the smile leaving his face. 'What's rattled your cage today?'

'What's wrong?' Charlie ranted. 'I'm talking about my basic human rights, the right to decide what I do, when I want to, choice of food, choice of the time I go to bed, or get up. Where I sit, or what I do.'

'Now just shut it and get up,' the nurse said angrily.

'You say you couldn't cope without discipline and a strict routine as there are not enough staff,' Charlie continued. 'And you insist that we do what we are told but, some of you encourage disobedience so that you can punish us.'

'There's no finer example than to have the pads full, to keep you on your toes,' responded the nurse.

'Keep us on our toes!' exclaimed Charlie. 'Some grubby little half-wit like you saying that to me. I know they are short of staff, but do they really never turn anybody down?'

Another 'pair of hands' arrived and Charlie was hauled off, to make his point by spending the rest of the morning in the pads, without any breakfast.

*****

Times were changing at the hospital. New ideas were being introduced into the wards, with the emphasis changing from containment to rehabilitation. Wards had been encouraged to unlock their doors and patients from one ward visited another ward to socialise. They played darts and took part in activities, such as playing Bingo.

Female staff were being introduced to male wards, a move that was not acceptable to all the male nurses. The first people in this venture were carefully chosen and placed on selected wards. Some patients also objected and would not let them near at first. It had always been said that the male wards, although clean and tidy, were regimental in the way things like furniture were assembled and placed. They lacked a women's touch, it was said, and sure enough things like ornaments and flowers started to appear. Patients whose chairs had been placed rigidly around the four corners of a room were placed in groups and facing each other. Someone suggested putting coloured counterpanes on the beds.

Another change was that the shift system was being queried. The female side worked twelve-hour shifts, 8am to 8pm, and the male wards did a shift of mornings, afternoons and nights, this was changed to the long day system.

The term 'therapeutic community' and 'therapeutic environment' was being used more and more. Our tutor explained these terms as, 'a hospital environment in which a conscious effort is made to employ all staff, and patient potential, in an overall treatment programme, according to the capacities and training of each individual member'.

But we are doing that already some of the charge nurses said.

'Yes,' they were told. 'You are, so let's see the evidence, write it down, evaluate it.'

Work was now becoming therapy. It was all too much for some. The staff on the long stay wards were told to look at each individual patient and assess his or her potential to be rehabilitated. At first they only had to categorise the patients into groups, identifying the higher achievers, the 'possibles' and the long stay. The long stay were those with dementia type illnesses, or extreme behavioural problems.

This was a big step in the changing attitudes towards mental illness, (psychiatric illness), and these changes were introduced in all the large mental hospitals throughout the country. There was also an emphasis on employing more staff to assist in therapies, and occupational therapists were beginning to take on an important role in rehabilitation. In fact, occupational therapists and social workers were being asked to assist in the assessment of some of the patients, though this did not go down well with a number of nurses who felt their own jobs were being undermined.

Some of the doctors were, more and more relying on the psychologist, to assist them in assessing and diagnosing patients. Others, however stubbornly kept to the old ways.

The entire culture of the hospital was changing and, in general terms, it wasn't easily accepted. It has often been stated that the entire structure of the traditional mental hospitals was managed in an authoritarian manner. As in any large institution, successful management depended on a full submission, with minimum amount of resistance, of the patients to the authority and this was only possible in the old days by the use of restraint, the threat of the pads, and keeping the sexes apart. As medication progressed, the use of sedation, continuous narcosis, and the threat of E.C.T. all, in some way, contributed to keeping everyone in line.

Patients were not encouraged to show the signs and symptoms of their illness and any outburst was quickly dealt with, so the emotions of fear, anxiety, frustration and boredom was curtailed to some degree.
Staff were also judged by their peers and superiors by the way they kept their ward. This meant having, at all costs, a quiet and tidy ward...promotion could often depend upon it. Some staff, if they spent a lot of time talking to the patients, were accused of being lazy, or even of 'skiving'.

Several patients on Charlie's ward were chosen as potential 'Rehabilitation material' and were referred to the hospital psychologist for assessment.
Charlie, who had redeemed himself following his outburst, which was put down to 'his frustration of not being able to achieve his full potential on this ward' was one of the first to visit.
The psychologist disturbed him.
'Where was he in his body?'
Charlie was perplexed.
'Where was he?'

'He was there, sitting down in his office,'
Charlie had replied.

'Yes, but where are you? Which part of you do
you identify yourself with? In which part of
your body do you reside?...your brain, your
heart, where?

Charlie had said he that he was in his head
because that is where you think and feel.

But was he?

Afterwards he lay on his bed and thought
about where he was in his body. He started
with his feet and worked upwards, trying to
find out where he was.

'Am I down there?' he shouted to his feet. He
waggled them about, but didn't feel he was in
his feet.

Was he in his legs?

He pinched them and although he felt it, he
certainly didn't feel he was there, even though
they were part of him.

He smiled to himself. Perhaps he was in his
bottom.

Charlie had heard that Freud had gone on
about people who were 'anal' and perhaps he
lived down there. But the smile soon left his
face, he wasn't there either, not that it

disappointed him too much that he was not up his own backside.

Up to his stomach. He didn't feel that he was there either. This was getting worrying.

Charlie started to get more agitated. He hadn't had such thoughts before and all he was asked to do was identify where he was in his body. He must be in his chest, his heart. That's it, he thought.

I must be in my heart, that's why you see arrows piercing the heart on valentine cards. Yes, that's where you feel you are when you are in love.

But as much as he tried, he could not find himself there either.

So he must have been right in the first place, he was located in his head. He must be there, but he didn't feel there at all.

Hell, where was he?

The psychologist was making him madder, instead of making him feel better, he thought.

'Nurse' where am I? I can't find myself anywhere,' he shouted leaping off his bed frightened, and running down the ward.

This little episode nearly led to him being removed from the rehabilitation list, but the staff kept faith in him, though his medication was reviewed.

Later when he had settled down, he returned to his bed, and lay down to have another think, as he called it.

You have got to say something about this place, he thought. If you are not mad when you come in, they certainly know how to 'cure' that. He certainly felt mad now. He didn't know who he was, where he was, or what he was! He didn't think much of the first phase of his rehabilitation programme.

On his next visit to the psychologist, Charlie had decided to reverse the roles and ask him where he was. That would show him.

The psychologist wasn't like the other staff he had become accustomed to. He was youngish man who wore spectacles and was dressed in a colourful jersey that looked two sizes too big for him. In fact, he looked scruffy to Charlie who was used to the nurses wearing smart uniforms. His hair was long and unkempt and he leaned lazily back in his chair sucking on an unlit pipe. His attitude was also different to what Charlie had expected. Instead of telling him what to do. He asked him his opinions, likes and dislikes. This had been off putting as he was no longer able to think for himself.

'Where are you?' he had asked the psychologist nervously.

'I'm here,' the psychologist replied. 'Right here in front of you, Charlie, Where did you think I was?'

'I know you are there,' Charlie replied. 'But where are you in your body?' he said cunningly.

'Why, I'm here, in all my body as a free thinking, feeling, sentient being, of course. Where are you?'

'I feel the same as you,' Charlie lied, hoping he had answered correctly.

'Good,' the psychologist said. 'Welcome back to the real world. Now let's move on.'

After a general chat about how Charlie had been, especially after having read the report on his behaviour following his previous visit, the psychologist decided to ask some more questions.

After asking him about his family and memories of his early childhood, the psychologist asked:

'If you were on a ship that was sinking out at

sea, Charlie, who would you evacuate first?'
He had been told this by his mother who had
always instilled in him how important women
were.

'Stand up, and give that lady your seat,' she
would say, even though the lady had not yet
got onto the bus. She said it in a loud voice to
show everyone else on the bus how well she
was bringing him up.

Open the door, carry her bags and boys always
go last if there were treats to be had.

Charlie certainly knew the answer to this
question.

'The women, and children, 'Charlie confidently
replied. 'Because women are more important
than men, and girls are more important than
boys.'

'Why do you think they are more important?'

'Because they are,' he replied. His mother was
always right he thought.

'Why?'

Hell, why is he asking me all these questions,
Charlie thought.

'They are more important because women are
the weaker sex and children are young and
need looking after and they have had less life

than me, so if anybody is going to drown, its me not them.'

'How often have you felt like drowning? he asked, sucking at his stupid pipe.

'Never,' Charlie replied.

'But you just said if anybody was going to drown it was you. Did you not think that after evacuating the women and children, you could evacuate the men and crew safely?' The psychologist suggested.

'No, I mean, yes. I don't know what I mean. I haven't had much time to think about the question,' Charlie stuttered.

The psychologist paused, making a sucking noise with his pipe. This was beginning to irritate Charlie, as he sat there feeling boxed in.

'Why do you think women are the weaker sex Charlie?' the psychologist continued, as if ready to apply the 'coup de grace'.

'Well they are, aren't they? Everybody knows that.'

'Weaker physically anyway,' he continued when he saw that the psychologist wasn't going to prompt him. Although his mother wasn't weak when she had beaten him, she wasn't from the weaker sex, he thought as he changed his mind.

'That's it, they are important because they have babies and are needed for reproduction,' he said gaining confidence.

'But aren't males important in the reproduction of the species,' the psychologist asked.

'Of course they are,' Charlie said, feeling angry and trapped.

'But one man could fertilise lots of women to protect the species,' he blurted out, ready to leave the room.

'How many women have you fertilised, Charlie?'......

Charlie woke up back in the 'box'. His head hurt, his buttocks hurt, and most of all his heart hurt, not physically but mentally.

How had it happened? he asked himself. One minute he had been allowed out of the ward to answer that stupid psychologist's questions and here he was banged up, back to square one.

He remembered being annoyed at the noise of the spit going up and down in the pipe as the 'shrink' stared at him with that superior look in his eyes.

That must have been why he had knocked the

pipe down his throat...when he had insulted him by accusing him of fertilising women. Well he won't be smoking that for a while, he thought with some degree of satisfaction. His mother had always told him to respect women, and practically suggested that sex was dirty. Surprisingly, he hadn't waited for the staff to come after he had injured the psychologist. In fact, it had been like a delayed reaction before they had boxed him up, as he had returned to the ward under his own steam. When they did come for him, he was sitting down, having a smoke which he realised would be his last for a while. He knew the routine and so got up and walked towards the pads.

They were heavy handed as usual, but not vicious. It was as if they had to push you, or shout at you, to assert their authority, even when you were co-operative.

They were even humorous when they gave him the 'unneeded' injection, as if pleased to see that he had sorted out 'that smart arsed shrink.'

'You always were the anal type Charlie,' a nurse said as they stuck the needle into his backside.

Occupational Therapy Department.

Occupational Therapy was first introduced to the hospital in 1933. It Provided a wide range of activities, organised in such a way as to ensure a proper balance between work, leisure and recreation.

Chapter fifteen.

My next move was to night duty and for my first experience of working at night I was allocated to a long stay ward. I knew that I would be working on my own, even though I was only a student nurse. Untrained staff and student's were left by themselves on this ward, supervised by the night charge nurse who made two visits, one before midnight and one to pick the ward report up the next morning. I soon settled down and after a few weeks preferred nights to day duty.

There were staff who did permanent nights and some had been on the same ward for many years.

Sitting there on my own with over fifty patients, all mentally ill, alone in the middle of the night, I had been asked by a friend if I was scared. In fact, I could not have felt safer. I was strangely comfortable and at peace with myself, sitting there in a dormitory. The fire would be roaring up the chimney and, usually, most of the patients would be sleeping peacefully, their rhythmic snoring competing with the wind in the chimney. Occasionally

one of them would sleepily plod off to the
toilet, or another would sneak off for a crafty
smoke. I soon knew who to trust, so there was
no need for me to get up; they would soon be
back in bed.

Patients who were a risk, potential 'fire
hazards' as they were known, had their
cigarettes and matches taken off them before
they went to bed, which were locked up in the
office until the morning. Their beds were often
searched to see if they had anything hidden in
them. Some of the patients were crafty at
concealing things in their pillow-cases and
mattresses. These patients were dangerous and,
left unobserved could set their beds alight.
They would sometimes steal from other
patients.

The art of being a good night nurse, was to
keep the place peaceful and quiet. Assert your
authority from the start. All in bed and lights
out the same time each night, so everyone
knew where they stood. Wake up those with
weak bladders around midnight, and send
them to the toilet, then there would be less wet
beds.

Let the trustees, like the kitchen man, stay up

an extra half hour as recognition of his standing in the pecking order on the ward. Then you would have no trouble, he would see to that, and he would bring you tea and toast in the morning.

Each ward had night lights that gave enough light for the nurse to see without any glare. I could see everybody from where I sat and patients could see their way to the toilet without bumping into another bed. The best way to disrupt a ward was to let someone fall onto someone else's bed. The ensuing cursing and shouting would wake everyone up and that would be the end of a peaceful night.

Another thing I had learned was to be aware of those patients who pilfered from the others. A fight was always guaranteed if someone was caught stealing from another patient. It was the ward policy to lock some of these difficult type of patient up in side rooms, if they were persistent offenders, or put them to sleep near the nurses observation post.

I was instructed to keep the restless patients up for an extra half hour, usually until their night sedation started to take effect. There was no point struggling with them and once they began to tire, you gave them a hot drink and settled them down.

Taking physical observations, like temperatures and blood pressure were rare on long stay wards, so unless their was an incident I used to write, 'all patients had a peaceful night, or just for a change 'all patients slept well.

The only problems I would expect to encounter would be epileptic fits and incontinence and as a student nurse I was expected to be able to cope with these problems.

Most epileptics were left to sleep off their fits, so as long as I ensured there was no obstruction to their airway, like their tongue being swallowed, or their face in the pillow, they presented no serious nursing problem. Incontinence in this age group was not uncommon during a fit, or sometimes a sedated patient would sleep 'deeply' not aware they were wetting the bed.

Tonight the coal bucket was full, and the fire was built up. No, I wasn't afraid. In fact, I couldn't think of a cosier place I'd rather be working in.

I was beginning not to think of being at work. It was becoming a way of life that I had become accustomed to. Perhaps I was getting institutionalised like the patients, but of course I hadn't been in the job long enough for that to happen, but some staff members had!

To add to my comfort the day staff had left me something for my supper. Tonight it was a chop, left over from the patients supper. Other times they had left eggs or a piece of cheese, so there was always something to eat. The custom of leaving the night staff food was due to the fact that there was not always enough staff on duty in the hospital to relieve you for your designated break, so it suited everybody if you ate on the ward.

One night charge would stay for a chat if I boiled him an egg, which was company during a twelve hour shift. He would tell me tales from times gone by as he had been here forty years. I was amazed at the amount of stories the older members of staff used to tell. They always called the old days the, 'good old days' and were continually reminiscing about the past.

I had been on nights for several weeks and had

been to different wards on several occasions. If I was on a ward with another nurse I was used as the supper relief. The only problem with this was I was last to supper and there was often nothing left to eat.

As I moved around I became aware that on nights there were a lot of ghost stories going around. On some of the wards I couldn't relax because of what I had heard.

There was the 'white lady' who walked around some of the female wards, not known to harm you but often a death followed her appearance. I heard about the 'clammy hand' that touched your face when you were relaxed in a chair and, needless to say I never relaxed on that ward. Then there was the 'toilet flusher'. On this ward something came and flushed all the toilets in the middle of the night.

One I didn't fancy meeting was the 'hanged man' who was said to walk the ward where he had been found hanging by a sheet in a sideroom many years ago.

Certain wards had reputations of mysterious happenings and my imagination was running wild before I even arrived on these wards. The older staff seemed to delight in warning you about these things, knowing you had to work on your own and that the only staff you would see all night was on your supper break, or the night charges fleeting visit.

My first experience of a ghost soon came and was on the refractory ward, Male one. There were two night staff on duty on this ward as most of these patients were unpredictable and some needed 'specialising'. The usual procedure was that one member of staff always remained in the dormitory, never leaving those patients on special observation out of their sight.

I was on my own as my colleague had gone on his supper break. We had done our rounds of the ward checking that everything was alright, and had put the night lights on. It was around 11:30pm and I was sitting in one of the two easy chairs at the bottom of the dormitory. I thought I heard someone walking up the corridor, and whoever it was appeared to be hitting the tables that lined the corridor, with something like a folded newspaper; it made a swishing sound. The noise got louder and louder and I expected someone to appear in the doorway at the top of the dormitory.

Instead I experienced something come in and walk down the dormitory and sit next to me. I didn't see it, just heard it and felt it. I froze, the hairs on the back of my neck stood out. I couldn't move and sweat ran down my brow. Then, whatever it was got up and I 'experienced' it go back up the dormitory and away down the ward.

I was shocked by this 'happening' and I never moved from my chair until my colleague returned. I felt unable to tell him what had happened to me in case he thought I was mad. I was very apprehensive working on that ward for a long time.

I did eventually share this experience with a friend and found out that there had been other incidents on this ward over many years. He told me that he had experienced that something was 'accompanying' him when he walked to the office. Other staff had thought that someone was opening the book cabinet during the night then sitting down in the day-room. It really was a spooky ward.

Ghosts were not the only things that disturbed my peace at night. On some wards the place became alive with pests as soon as the lights went out. Although the grounds were full of feral cats, they rarely came inside and so most wards had mice running around. One night I went into the kitchen and as I put the light on I saw a mouse scampering around the water boiler. In its haste to escape it fell in. One male nurse who was afraid of mice tucked his trouser legs into his socks when he was on duty in case one ran up his leg! The worse pests were cockroaches. On some wards they were everywhere and they would crunch under your feet as you walked about. Nothing seemed to kill them and they would be everywhere one minute, but would miraculously disappear as soon as it got light.

*****

Some patients who had spent may years living in the mental hospital behaved as if they were suffering from chronic illness, such as schizophrenia, or dementia. This was mainly due to them living in the institution for all those years without the necessary mental stimulation to prevent them from becoming listless, apathetic, and unresponsive. They did what they were told, had little choice in what they did on each particular day, and ate what was put in front of them. The wards were run on a strict routine and everything was done by the clock, from the time they got up until they went to bed.

Charlie did his time in seclusion, which was only for one night, and was then allowed to join the patients in the ward again. He had half-heartedly apologised for his actions which showed that he was at least learning to think more rationally, although he could not understand how he had got himself worked up into such a state in the first place. Surprisingly, his name had not been taken off the rehabilitation list; he was not the first choice for the scheme with some members of the staff, but he was still there with a chance. Although Charlie had promised himself not to become like some of the other patients on the ward, especially those he had seen walking about like zombies, he was unable to prevent himself from slowly sinking into a kind of dejected apathy on this ward.

He was bored and now that he was 'grounded again' he had very little physical exercise. The less he did, the less he wanted to do.

There was a book cabinet on the ward, but the books had been there for years. Not that they were not changed periodically, but they were always another wards set of old books. The only time he had seen them put to good use was when a patient dared to tear out a page to make or light a cigarette.

It was even getting to the stage when Charlie was resentful towards the staff who told him to get a shave, or a wash, or change his clothes. At first he thought, 'what's the point? Now he couldn't even be bothered to look after his personal hygiene. He didn't even want to go out to the limited visits to the shop and, especially, not to that awful dance they held on Monday evenings, although at one time he used to enjoy them.

To Charlie, unlike most of the other patients, the dance, instead of being enjoyed, had become a nightmare. He had never mixed well as a child and hated to be the centre of attention. To be told to get up, and sometimes be dragged up, to dance with some stupid women who dribbled all over him, blew smoke in his face, and stood on his feet, was not his idea of fun.

One patient even fancied him and kept pestering him to come outside for sex, but the feeling was certainly not mutual.

Sex was something he had no experience of at all, well except for masturbating which most of them did on the ward. What else could they do? He was aware of the odd act of homosexuality in the toilets and had heard some patients having 'secret' sex with the women in the grounds. But really he just wasn't interested, although he had often wondered what it would be like to have sexual intercourse, but he wasn't that desperate to find out, especially with this one.

It was not that he objected to others enjoying themselves at the dance. When he had been 'well' he had been impressed by the way some of them had danced and had attended voluntary, but now it was the lack of choice that got to him.

'Get your suit on, your going to the dance,' he would be told.

There had never been a choice in anything you did on this ward. Now it was worse as he had been told that patients on the rehabilitation scheme would attend all the social functions that were held in the hospital.

Charlie had never been keen on the man who organised the dance, he irritated him with his antics.

'He will be next for the 'pipe treatment', he thought. He wasn't a nurse; he didn't know what he was. He did not seem to understand that everybody didn't feel like the joys of spring every day, as he apparently did.

He announced the dances as if he was at the Quaintway's ballroom, in town. He then jigged up and down, or clapped his hands with such enthusiasm, Charlie felt sick. He was always smiling, but somehow always managed to look miserable. He tried to inspire everyone around him, but he certainly had the knack of doing the opposite to Charlie.

Fortunately for Charlie, he had not been in the hospital long enough to become institutionalised. He was just 'flat', depressed, and had no goal in life other than to survive another long day.

The staff who had been selected to run the rehabilitation scheme had begun to realise the effects of apathy and boredom on these patients, especially the ones who were capable of logical thinking. They were enthusiastically preparing a programme to cater for their individual needs.

There had always been activities in the hospital, but these had either been mainly work related, or designed for mass entertainment. The only occupational therapy available was focused on the acute patients who were on the admission wards.

This scheme was going to be different. It was structured to get some of the patients out, at least out of the wards, and hopefully some out of hospital.

A staff meeting was held and the patients were carefully selected as to who would be suitable to participate and gain the most benefit.

Charlie, being classed as a 'new long stay' patient, was one of the eight chosen, but he had blotted his copy book by his violent behaviour towards the psychologist.

The psychologist, although bruised from the encounter, still saw the potential in Charlie to achieve more than he was doing. To his credit he didn't allow the incident to change his mind about Charlie. In fact he put it down to his frustrations at being incarcerated in the hospital against his will. He had been shocked by the fact that Charlie, and some of the other patients he had interviewed were in a long stay ward and he was keen to start the programme. Some of the older staff belittled his views about Charlie, saying if had injured them he wouldn't have seen daylight again this year. There was some opposition to the scheme, mostly from the same source who opposed Charlie being included.

Some members of staff wanted to make sure that the 'favoured' patients would not take up most of their time to the detriment of the other patients on the ward which, they argued, would further their slide into oblivion.

There was also those who saw this as a threat to their own professional status and did little to co-operate at all, stating that the nurses were handing over their professional expertise to the occupational therapists and psychologists.

Others had heard Enoch Powell, the Minister of Health state that these large Victorian institutions would be closed within twenty years. It was his intention to 'the elimination of by far the greater part of this country's mental hospitals as they stand today'. In his famous 'Water Tower' speech he had said, 'There they stand, isolated, majestic, imperious, brooded over by the gigantic water tower and chimney combined, rising unmistakable and daunting out of the countryside, the asylums which our forefathers built with such immense solidity.' This speech had been rebuked by some of the staff as rubbish, but now they were changing their tune as the rehabilitation schemes commenced.

The first phase of the programme started with eight patients, (later it would include hundreds) and it was agreed the success of the programme would be measured by any improvements showed by the patients each month. The patients were given beds in the same area of the dormitory, with the emphasis being placed on improvement of personal hygiene and interacting with each other. They were issued with their own soap, tooth brush and toilet bag and given new lockers, a novelty for some who had been used to putting their clothes in a bundle under their bed.

A budget was made available to purchase new clothes and a weekly allowance to go out on visits or shopping.

Each morning, Charlie and his new colleagues were encouraged to wash and shave, then sit together for their breakfast. Table cloths and crockery were provided and the patients were encouraged to clear their tables and wash up. At first there was some resentment shown towards these patients by some members of staff. One in particular tried to goad Charlie when no one else was in earshot.

'Have you wiped your bum properly?' and 'Hello Charlie, who taught you to use a knife and fork?

The members of staff selected to run the programme soon realised that the old habits of some staff members were never going to change and that they could not successfully mix the old with the new. It was agreed that a new location should be found, and be known as the rehabilitation unit.

*****

It became quite a shock to me when I discovered some of the jobs that I would be expected to take on as a nurse. Many of them

were not the kind of tasks I had envisaged
when I had decided to make nursing my career
choice.

There were the cleaning duties on the ward,
such as scrubbing, mopping, and cleaning
windows. Then there had been the tasks I had
been required to do as a cadet nurse, like
sewing buttons on trousers, pressing clothes
and washing up dishes in the staff kitchen.
There was a heavy work load on the long-stay
ward that I was allocated to, with eighty
patients to care for. After a long day out with
the barrow gang they all had to be shaved by
three members of staff each evening. The
patients were bathed weekly and in between
bath days they all had to be supervised with
their washing as the work they did was hard
and sweaty. I could never understand why they
were only allowed one bath each week.

There were sometimes up to forty patients on
this big gang that went down to the fields from
this ward, and four or five on the smaller ones,
that cleaned the grounds, chopped wood, and
delivered coal. My first day on the barrow
gang was a real eye opener. There were three
large carts that had to be pulled down to the

fields.

The patients on the ward assembled in the boot room after breakfast where they changed their shoes for strong hob nailed boots. For identification purposes each pair of shoes and boots had a number made in brass tacks which the cobbler had hammered into the soles. The same number was on the patients clothes, and suits. They had two suits, the best one worn on Sundays and visiting time.

The boot room had numerous pairs of boots on shelves and overcoats and caps hung from hooks around the room. I imagined the chaos that would ensue if the boots weren't numbered.

Once dressed in their working clothes, the patients collected their working tools; brushes, shovels, spades and hoes; then they lined up in pairs to form a long line outside.

Two of them picked up large tea urns and headed off towards the main kitchen where they would be filled up with hot tea. They would also pick up the rations, consisting of freshly baked loaves of bread and a huge piece of cheese which we all ate on our mid-morning break.

A patient got between the shafts of each of the large two-wheeled carts, whilst others went to the sides or back of them to push. Everyone seemed to know what their role was and I was surprised how such a big gang of mentally ill men organised themselves with little prompting from the staff.

I thought it an impressive sight when the gang moved off. I felt I was in some kind of a parade and fantasised about being in charge of all these men. A fine bunch of men they were, I thought as we marched them off. One nurse in front, then the first cart, a few of the men then the second cart, followed by another nurse, more men, then myself and a few more men followed the last cart.

'Get them brushes up on your shoulders,' I ordered my men at the back. 'Backs straight; left, right, left, right, keep in line up there.'

I suddenly returned to earth as the dust started getting into my mouth and I realised that as in the army, the lowest in rank followed the muck carts.

Not deterred for long by these thoughts, I was soon cheerful again, as I was glad to be out in the fresh air, instead of being confined to a hot and busy ward all day.

We were working in the Willows which was out of the hospital grounds, through the farm, and across two fields. The first part of the gang stopped at the farm to fill their barrows with manure and pig muck which they would spread onto the fields. The remainder of us carried on until we arrived at the brick shack which was our base. The last fifty yards of our walk was along a line of tall popular trees waving in the breeze. It was a beautiful place to work with the sun shining and the birds singing. I later found out that it was not so enjoyable on the wet and cold days when the work still had to be done.

We stopped and set up our base. The patients knew the routine and started digging, some began weeding while others were just there as they had nothing else to do. Nobody cared as long as they were out of the ward.

One of the nurses showed me how to prepare a patch to grow cabbages.

At 10am the 'tea men' arrived with the hot tea which was served in mugs, old cups and even jam jars. I was given a thick piece of bread and an even thicker piece of cheese, by a patient who had filthy hands and I didn't fancy eating it, but I did, it was delicious, and I looked forward to this break every time I was on the gang.

For lunch we had to return to the ward, a good fifteen minutes walk away. All the patients had to change their boots, eat their dinner and then after half an hours rest, when they smoked or dozed in a chair, it was back to the Willows. Everyone was habitually counted and the ward was informed of how many we were taking out, as the numbers varied due to the patients behaviour or other appointments.

Once back at the Willows the patients got on with their work, until the afternoon break of tea and cake.

There was no room for any fads here as again I hesitated when I saw how the cups had been washed.

If it was wet or windy we would put a cart on its side for shelter. At 4-30pm we headed back to the ward. The patients were lined up until we could account for every tool we had taken with us.

I was really tired even though I hadn't done much more than supervise the patients and their work, so was really dismayed when the charge nurse told us to start shaving before supper. I was shown how to shave each patient with five strokes of the razor. The barber who had trained me would have gone mad, but he didn't have to shave all these patients in an hour. Some shaved themselves while we continually shaved a row of patients who sat in chairs. They had either lathered themselves with the brush and soap from three communal shaving mugs, or were lathered by one of the patients helping us. We really did get into a rhythm and were finished in time for supper. Some of the patients liked to go to bed after supper and we had to lock the dormitory door to keep them up. If we let them go to bed too early they would be up early and wandering around the ward for half the night.

Others preferred a game of snooker, some helped wash up, but most just dozed off in the chair. The lucky ones the hard workers, or the undernourished were given a bottle of Guinness or Pale Ale.

Lights out was at 10pm.

Chapter sixteen.

Ambrosia was the nickname given to a tramp who used to sleep rough in town. He got his name from the habit of sitting on the pavement in the shopping area of town and eating cold rice pudding from the tin. In appearance he seemed to be of medium height, stocky, with long grey hair. He had an even longer beard which was also turning grey.

Ambrosia had been hanging around town for several months and was often seen chasing some of the local youths who found it funny to mock and upset him. He would charge after them, sometimes knocking shoppers over, and was surprisingly agile for his age. He would shout abuse and swear, and was sometimes quite aggressive.

In his quieter moments he would 'entertain' passers-by with renditions of Irish folk songs, or by dancing a jig, which was rather surprising as he was found to be from South Wales.

Charlie first came across Ambrosia when he was hauled through the door, shouting abuse at the staff who were transferring him into his ward.

He found out through the bush telegraph, which even patients had access to, that Ambrosia had been brought to the hospital by the police who were fed up with his behaviour in town. They had sought his compulsory admission to hospital and one look at him had convinced the psychiatrist that he should be on a long stay ward. He had remained in the admission ward for no longer than it had been needed to fill in the paperwork.

Charlie knew a colourful character when he saw one and so got up from his chair and, not wishing to miss the fun, followed the nurses and Ambrosia down the ward.

Ambrosia was told to sit down. He was bellowing at the staff that he was not bloody mad and was not staying here. The charge nurse, having been disturbed from the comforts of his office by the noise, strolled down the ward. He put on his glasses, in a slow and meaningful manner, to inspect Ambrosia. From a distance he examined him from head to toe, and with an expression of disgust on his face declared: 'He's bloody lousy, he'll infect the whole bloody ward.'

Two nurses were told to take him immediately down the 'backs' and sort him out.

Unfortunately for Charlie, he was too nosey for his own good and being the nearest patient was instructed to give them a hand. He couldn't protest as the order was given by the charge nurse whose word was never disobeyed by anybody, without serious consequences.

'It will be good for your rehabilitation,' the charge nurse said as he sauntered back to the office.

Helping in this case meant handling all the dirty clothes; the nurses didn't want to be infested. Ambrosia was dragged protesting down to the bathroom where he was told to strip. He refused and so Charlie was told to undress him. This was not achieved without Charlie being abused by the tramp who had guessed he wasn't a nurse.

'Get your hands off me you mad bastard,' he had shouted at Charlie, who struggled to untie a knot in the string that kept the tramp's clothes together.

At the same time blows rained around Charlie's ears, much to the delight of the staff. Charlie had never seen so many layers of

clothes on one person. Under the filthy black
overcoat was a jacket, then a jersey, a pullover,
shirt and vest.

These were all matted with dirt and he
imagined he could see fleas jumping.

Ambrosia kicked and screamed while the staff
held him down to enable Charlie to pull of his
boots and fell back laughing when he was
overwhelmed by the smell.

'I'm not touching those,' Charlie said, staring at
the threadbare socks.

'He'll need an anaesthetic to get them off,' a
nurse said, sarcastically.

'Get them off, or you'll go in the bath with him,
the other nurse ordered, but even he relented
when he saw the size of the tramps toe nails
which were sticking out of the holes in his
socks.

By the nearest thing to a non touch technique,
Ambrosia was unceremoniously thrown into
the bath of disinfected water. Charlie was
soaked by the wave of water that came over
the back of the bath and obeyed the order to
start scrubbing as the nurse held Ambrosia
down. There was water everywhere and
Charlie's skin crawled from the thought of the

fleas that must be on him.

He also marvelled as to how thin the tramp looked now that he was naked. In fact, after a haircut and his beard shaved off, Ambrosia looked small and pathetic, stripped of his identity. Standing there shaking from the loss and comfort of his warm fleecy coat, he reminded Charlie of a sheep after it had been dipped and sheared. Charlie was told to hold the tramp while the nurses sprayed him with D.D.T. Powder. There was nearly as much powder on Charlie as there was on Ambrosia as the nurse pumped away with his 'Flit' like pump and soon they could see the little monsters falling on to the newspaper he was standing on. The next job was to dispose of all the clothes, for burning, and Charlie was given the task of going through the pockets. These were stuck together and he had to force his hand in, as Ambrosia was shouted abuse at him. 'Get out of my pockets, you thieving bastard,' he screamed.

And Charlie soon understood why for inside he found a bungle of notes which when counted amounted to nearly £10. He had enough to have bought himself some new clothes.

At teatime, it was a different Ambrosia who presented himself for the ward to see. He was a smaller version of the person who was admitted and he looked thinner in his hospital issue of jacket and trousers. His spirit had also gone, to some degree, as he limped to the table in his new pair of shoes, his feet hurting following the 'surgery' on his nails.

Instinctively, because he was the only face he recognised, he looked to Charlie to show him the ropes.

His name was Tim and he soon recovered from his unexpected exile to start his jigging and singing, a trick that had served him well in the past, and it made the nurses to laugh, enabling him to stand out and gain attention in this overcrowded environment.

It amazed Charlie how quickly Ambrosia, a knight of the road, settled down in the confined space of the ward. In fact, he was bossing the other patients around, calling them names, and some were responding to his demands.

Ambrosia was not the only tramp to be admitted to the hospital. Anybody who was homeless and hung around town too long was in danger of being 'certified'. This was more likely if the miscreant was a nuisance or noticeable, as Ambrosia had been by his antics. Some of the tramps were alcoholics and the withdrawal was sometimes too extreme for them, especially if the doctor did not have insight into their medical history. Apart from beer and spirits, some were known to drink turpentine when they couldn't get anything else.

Charlie had once seen a patient go outside and haul up a bottle of 'turps' from a grid where it had been tied. The patient had taken a long swig and then lowered it back down until he needed another drink. It amused Charlie that someone had got one over on the staff, and so he had said nothing.

The new alcoholic patients who could not get a drink often became seriously ill. They were sometimes already physically ill with a vitamin B deficiency, cirrhosis of the liver, or peripheral neuritis. They often suffered from the D.T.s (delirium tremens), and ended up on the sick ward where they would be treated for dehydration, salt depletion, and vitamin deficiencies. They may also have been prescribed tranquillisers and anti-convulsants. Patient's often 'felt' that things like spiders were crawling over them and they also 'saw' things, hence the 'pink elephant' comments.

Charlie got to like Ambrosia, but could only tolerate being in his company for short periods of time as he got on his nerves. He wouldn't answer to his nickname, telling everyone his name was Tim, Although Charlie noticed that there was no objection to him being called Ambrosia when there were cigarettes to be had.

Ambrosia soon became part of the furniture, as they say. Charlie was more concerned with his own life and was encouraged by the staff to keep up with his rehabilitation programme. 'Got to stay on the top table!' a nurse would say, alluding to his place at meal times.

*****

Following a two-week session at the training school, I moved to Male 7 which was situated in the main building, immediately below Male

5.

I was, once again, allocated to work here for three months, and it specialised in nursing the physically ill and elderly patients. It was one of four wards in the hospital in which patients with Pulmonary Tuberculosis,
(T.B.) were nursed on specially designated verandah's. I had been told that in the 50's and 60's most of the large mental institutions had cases of T.B. and here was no exception.
Male 7 had a large, airy verandah which stretched along the whole length of its south wall and catered for up to ten cases of T.B. The other patients on the ward were either the frail elderly or physically ill, most suffering from chronic heart and chest complaints. There was also a ward, for the acutely ill and post operative cases, situated in the Annexe part of the hospital.
Some patients on this ward were classified as quiescent T.B. cases, i.e patients who had been treated for tuberculosis and were now no longer 'active cases'.
On recovery some of these patients stayed on the ward to assist staff caring for those nursed on the verandah.

On commencing their employment at the hospital, all staff who were likely to come in contact with these patients were given a Mantoux test, to identify if they were required vaccinating against T.B. A failure of the skin to react to this test, usually seen as a small eruption on the forearm made it necessary for them to have a B.C.G (Bacille Calmette Guerin) vaccination. It was the policy of the hospital to employ a proportion of staff who were registered as being disabled, known as 'green card' holders. Some of these people had recovered from T.B. and were recruited specifically to work on this type of ward.

Any patient who contracted T.B. within the hospital was transferred to one of these specially designated wards. The remaining patients and staff of that ward would be be screened.

The verandah's where the patients were nursed were unbearably hot at the height of summer and cold in the winter, as the windows were left open to let the fresh air in that was recommended as being beneficial for these patients. Because these patients were nursed in isolation from the other patients on the ward, the verandah had its own toilets, bathroom and kitchen, and all the utensils were kept separate. The ward kitchen man, was a patient called Joe, who was a quiescent T.B. Case, and he was responsible for a great deal of the duties in this area. He gave out the nourishing drinks and bottle's of stout in the evening.

The treatment for T.B. included prolonged bed rest, physiotherapy, and a combination of three drugs, Streptomycin, P.A.S. and Isoniazid.

All cases of T.B. were notifiable, and a Chest Physician not the Psychiatrist was responsible for the treatment of these patients. The favoured meal for the sick and frail patients was known as 'pobs'. This was a special way of making bread and milk, and Joe, who was an expert in making this dish, showed me how to make it. He broke the bread up into small pieces, including the crusts, and put it into a large metal pot; he then added just enough milk to make it stodgy, followed by glucose and Complan and a few raw eggs. All this was left to simmer on the stove for a while and stirred regularly, adding more milk as required. When ready the pobs were put into bowls to cool and more sugar and glucose was added.

This dish was given to the sick and frail patients as their main meal.

I found the nursing care to be of a high standard on this and other sick wards. Some of the nurses had returned from the local general hospital where they had been seconded to qualify as General nurses, so were double trained; R.M.N and S.R.N. Others had a special aptitude towards sick nursing, so stayed on this ward rather than the refractory wards where brawn rather than brain was said to be the main requirement.

There was a great deal of specialised nursing taking place here, as patients were rarely transferred to a general hospital.

There were over fifty patients on this ward, and most of them slept in the main dormitory which contained four rows of tightly packed beds.

Many of these patients had physical illness's such as bronchitis, or congestive heart failure. Some had large ulcers or bedsores, and needed morphine before they were treated. Other's were catheterized, and they all had symptoms of mental illness, such as confusion or senile dementia.

The patients were washed and shaved after breakfast and those who were able were got up to sit in a large semi circle of Offerton chairs around the fireplace. Most of the patients who were in bed wore night shirts and those allowed up wore the distinctive multi coloured dressing gowns of the hospital.

The main sick ward for the hospital was situated in the Annexe. Here, with the operating theatre near by, they nursed surgical cases. There was plenty opportunities to practice your bandaging skills here, which were essential to pass the practical parts of your exams.

During the second world war this part of the hospital was taken over by the military to treat the casualties of war.

Patients who required psychosurgery were sent to Rainhill hospital, near Liverpool. These were mainly pre-frontal leucotomies which was often the preferred procedure for disturbed patients not responding to their current treatment. I was surprised when I learnt how the insane had been treated in the early days, the surgery then was very much a hit or miss affair and many patients were left as 'cabbages', devoid of personality or motivation.

I was told that today this operation could account for as many positive results as failures.

In an annual report, 13/3/1957, it was stated: *Our first leucotomy operation was in 1947 and since then 184 patients have had this brain operation. It enabled 101 patients to leave this hospital whose discharge would not otherwise have been possible. The introduction of the new tranquillising group of drugs has reduced the number of operations without replacing the need for leucotomy in some cases. For several years about 30 patients a year have had this operation. There existed a backlog of longer stay patients, some of whom could benefit from leucotomy, but now most cases have been sifted out, and we did only 5 operations in 1955, and 6 in 1956. Of these 11 leucotomies, four patients have been discharged as recovered, and 2 have improved, and 5 have shown no improvement at all.*

It was a common sight in the hospital to see patients who had endured this operation and had been left with unmistakable scars, i.e. round hollows on either side of their foreheads, about an inch in diameter. One patient had told me that was where his horns had been when he was the devil.

*****

I was on a long-stay ward on the Sunday that the main hall caught fire. The charge nurse, who was the bleep holder for the fire watch that day had gone home for his lunch, and left the bleep with me. Nothing would happen he had assured me as he left the ward.
It was the hospital routine to identify a person who would take charge of such matters especially at weekends, and all wards were aware of who it was.
Ten minutes after the charge nurse had left the ward the bleep went off and a fire alert came over.
'Fire in the main hall!' Fire in the main hall!' the telephonist's voice cried.
Although it was not a ward area, it was a place where some of the patients, and their visitors met at the weekend, so I hurried off, leaving the other nurses on their own.

Not used to being in charge, I was alarmed that I was involved, but reassured myself with the thought that it would probably be a false alarm, which often happened. At worst I thought it might be a cigarette end left burning by a patient, not an uncommon occurrence either. However, I was stunned by the scene, and when I saw the smoke in the corridor I realised we were dealing with a major fire. The first thing I saw was the porter and a workman from the boiler house, directing the fire hose to the pharmacy end of the hall. It was well alight.

I moved up the corridor, to the side entrance, and was horrified. The wood-panel walls and the curtains were on fire. There appeared to be no one inside and I could see Ray, the porter, tackling the fire at the far door. The heat was unbearable, so much so that the chairs were melting and changing shape before my eyes. The fire seemed to stand still for a moment, just dancing up the panelled walls and catching the curtains on the top windows. The stage curtains were also on fire.

I again checked from a distance that there was nobody inside, but soon moved backwards as the fire brigade had arrived...just as the whole stage area went up in flames.

I discussed a strategy with some of the staff who had arrived to make sure that no patients or visitors were in the hall and to be doubly sure, the firemen searched the area in their breathing suits. We rang all the hospital wards to tell them what was happening and asked them to account for all their patients. This took quite some time as some patients were walking in the grounds. The nurse in charge of the hospital arrived and took charge of the situation, much to my relief.

As this was a major fire all the senior personnel were called in, and extra staff were drafted in to help cope.

Everyone else just stood around dumbfounded. It was a major shock to see such a beautiful building being destroyed by fire. Staff off duty just came in to be there... they could not believe what was happening.

Later I was severely shocked by the experience, but never told anyone. In fact I was treated as if I was never there; others told there own stories which were exaggerated more and more each time they were told.

The shock of the fire stayed with me and was the most frightening experience of my career so far, but worse experiences were to follow.......just seeing those flames reducing that grand hall, which had earlier seemed so invincible to a heap of debris; thank God no one was seriously hurt.

*****

Charlie was enjoying his newly found freedom that went with his rehabilitation course and was responding well to the stimulation the training was giving him. He was now clean and tidy in appearance, and, with his improved social skills, was able to to satisfy the staff that he was fit for parole outside the grounds. He was generally feeling and looking a lot better. The one activity he still resented was the weekly patient's dance....he had been one of the last patients to be accounted for on the day of the fire, as he was sitting in the bushes watching the smoke billowing up to the sky. One of the staff had said he had seen Charlie in the hall during the morning and for a while staff were afraid for his safety.....

Chapter seventeen.

Two revolutionary things happened in the
hospital that year, and they were to have a
major impact on Charlie's life. First, it was
decided to convert an old hall on the perimeter
of the grounds, to accommodate all the
patients who were deemed as suitable for a
rehabilitation programme leading to
Community care.
Second, it was decided that six patients would
be 'employed' as ward orderlies, and help with
general duties on selected wards.
Charlie and his colleagues in the 'rehab' group
were the first to move into the new
accommodation which was known as Bache
hall. They each had their own room, with a
bed, wardrobe and chest of drawers, the latter
being a novelty for Charlie as he had been
used to bundling his clothes into a small
locker. Charlie's room was situated on the first
floor and overlooked a large garden which was
kept in immaculate condition by a patient who
had worked here, and on the Bache farm for
years. He too moved into the new
accommodation. He kept himself to himself,

appearing to be aloof towards the other patients and only really communicated with the staff. This perceived aloofness was mainly due to his deafness, and that for years he had been treated as staff.

Charlie was delighted with his room and was encouraged to buy his own things to give it the personal touch. Staff brought in bric-a-brac to help make the rooms more homely.

The Bache Hall scheme was unique in that there was to be both male and female patients living together, and supervised by male and female staff.

When the first female patients arrived, it was noticeable that, the men sat in one side of the room and the women the other. Gradually, new relationships developed and both sexes integrated well. Men started to take more pride in their appearance, as did the women.

Charlie could not believe his luck when he was told that he was to start work as an orderly on his old ward; Monday to Friday and Saturday mornings.

Most of the patients who had moved into Bache hall were already working in the hospital. They were employed in areas such as the laundry, shop, farm, gardens, and the works departments.

Some of the senior nursing staff complained bitterly when they discovered that their 'best' patients were being moved into Bache Hall as they were considered by them to be part of the ward's unofficial workforce. A compromise was reached and some of the patients were allowed back to these wards during the day. It was also partly due to the movement of these patients that the decision was taken to employ ward orderlies.

Charlie's day began at 7am when he got up and washed before breakfast. He would leave for work early as it was a ten minute walk to the wards from Bache Hall. He had to walk across a path between two fields growing vegetables, and staff would ask him to bring back a cabbage or some sprouts, which he often did. On wet and windy days the patients got soaked, or nearly blown away, but most of the time they were glad to be out with their thoughts and feelings driving them on to work. On the ward he would make a brew of tea, then organise the washing up of the dishes. His other duties included taking charge of the kitchen, mopping the floors, cleaning out the toilets, and generally keeping the ward tidy. He had his dinner on the ward and remained there until the tea dishes were done, usually getting back to Bache hall around six pm, where he had his supper.

At first his duties were very demanding as he was not nearly fit enough for a man of his age, he was still on fairly heavy medication and had previously led a sedentary life on the wards for several years.

All he wanted to do when he had eaten his supper was listen to the radio or sleep. Unfortunately, this was not an option for the enthusiastic   rehabilitation team of staff.

'Come on Charlie, time for the quiz,' or, 'are you ready for the dance?'

The dance had been resurrected in the Annexe hall, nearly a mile away, as it was on the other side of the hospital. Some of the patients were worn out after their days work and were reluctant to join in with these evening activities. Charlie had to make his bed, tidy his room, which had to be cleaned properly at the weekend. Then there was cooking; plan your

own meal, cook it, serve it, eat it, wash up.
Charlie was beginning to think if this 'rehab
lark' was a good thing after all.

There were daily group activities for those
who didn't work, with the new occupational
therapists, remedial gymnast, and social skills
teacher all demanding a piece of the patients
time.

Fortunately, one of the old hands recognised
the burden's placed on some of the patients, so
the programme was changed to give working
patients more 'free' time.

Charlie was issued with a brown suit, a symbol
of authority to him, and half a dozen white
aprons. And although he had been at his job
for several weeks he still felt continually tired.
He would cat-nap behind the pantry door and
abused any patient who wandered in and
disturbed him.

Charlie knew how to keep the charge nurse
sweet. He took him hourly cups of tea and set
aside a dinner for him before the patients were
served. He also kept watch, just in case the
Chief Male Nurse appeared. However, the
Chief was nobody's fool and would sometimes
look into the oven and ask Charlie who the

dinner was for. Charlie would lie, saying it was for a patient at X-ray, but the chief was satisfied that he had made his point, he was in charge, and he could stop that 'practice' any time he chose.

The scheme for the use of orderlies on the wards had been a success, and their duties now included running messages, so they were given a pass key.

The key was to be left on the ward at the end of each shift.

Charlie gradually took over the responsibilities for collecting the ward post, took specimens to the path lab, and ran messages for the staff and patients who wanted items from the shop, and he even placed their bets.

He was often rewarded with a cigarette or some loose change.

The next thing that effected Charlie's welfare was that he was transferred from the care of Dr Minor, to the care of the Consultant in charge of the rehabilitation programme, Dr Malstead. Charlie met Dr Malstead and two of the team members to discuss his future. He was apprehensive and suspicious of their motives, as they asked about his family. He had had no contact with them since his admission and following a visit by a social worker was told that they were hostile towards him going home on weekend leave. Generally there had been a mixed response for patients who were to be rehabilitated into the community. Some patients had been in the hospital that long that their next of kin had died, or their old addresses no longer existed.

Charlie was classed as a new-long stay patient and his situation was seen as promising, in spite of his history and family background. He told the doctor that he was happy in his current situation.

Dr Malstead asked, 'how do you see your future Charlie?'

'Future?' Charlie muttered. Until recently, Charlie had thought he had no future in this place, and became anxious because he couldn't answer the question.

The doctor reassured him, and told him he was doing well, and to go and think about his future, which they would discuss at their next meeting.

*****

I was allocated to the admission ward, Male 12, to help me prepare for my exams. Male 12 was where the patients in the acute phase of their illnesses were nursed, with textbook signs and symptoms, it was one of the most important wards for a student nurse to gain experience on.

Here the manics were manic. Their clothes sometimes decorated with jewellery or flowers, and they were as 'high as kites', they never kept still nor stopped talking from the moment they came in. On the other hand, the depressed were low, non-communicating, and often suicidal, and it was remarkable to witness how they improved after starting treatment with E.C.T. The charge nurse told me to be vigilant with observing these patients as after several treatments they may be capable of acting out their suicidal thoughts.

The aggressive patient would often come in fighting. I saw one chap, handcuffed, and brought in by six policeman. They undid his cuffs and then cleared off, leaving us to cope. We had been taught that when dealing with aggressive people, we should remain calm, relaxed and not react to insults etc... in this case it was a case of all hands on deck and into the box, where we all got a clout taking the clothes off him, no complaints, just part of the job!

The staff on this ward were all rank conscious, each wearing epaulettes, on the shoulders of their white coats.

I was reminded of never repeating anything about the patients away from the ward, as one was a famous footballer. The atmosphere on the ward was one of strictness and efficiency. To me, the inexperienced student, there was a feeling of insecurity, you never knew who was coming through the door next. One person who did amaze me was the Consultant Psychiatrist, Dr Minor. He would never deal with anyone but the charge nurse, or his deputy; and one of them always had to be on duty for his ward visits. No-one else had an opinion worth listening to, and patients symptoms when described by a nurse were often ignored. The junior staff on day and night duty were privy to everything that went on, but if the charge nurse did not include their observations in his report, they were ignored. Dr Minor would never change his opinions on the way he treated the mentally ill.

I learned policies and procedures relating to the admission of patients and the sections of the Mental health act 1959 which were particularly relevant to admission and discharge.

Section 36 was an interesting part of the act as it related to patients correspondence and communication. It permitted the R.M.O. to withhold distressing or threatening letters to and from patients though regulations did not apply to the Minister of Health, a patients M.P., legal authorities or the hospital management committee.

Some patients wrote 'rubbish', or complained about their plight and it was not uncommon to see a letter addressed to the Queen.

New admissions were nursed in bed and kept under strict observation. I sat with a trained nurse for the first few days to learn what to do. This was similar to the approach on the refractory ward where some of their patients were under observation, known as being 'on the book'.

Blue and red cards signified the degree of observation a patient was on and the nurse was obliged to sign the back to show they were responsible for that patient. A blue card meant special observation was required, a red card meant that the patient was a suicidal risk, and were never allowed to be out of a nurses sight. An experienced nurse told me that a true suicidal patient would often succeed in killing themselves eventually. Asking him what he meant by a 'true suicide' he said, that some patients attempted to harm themselves as a superficial gesture to manipulate a situation, but some times things went wrong and they killed themselves. He called these the 'scratchers', explaining that a small number of patients cut their wrist with regular frequency, but never far away from the public eye. A true suicide often went to a private place and finished the job off properly.

Statistics revealed that gassing was the most common method of suicide in Britain, followed by poisoning, hanging, drowning, then self inflicted injuries.

The nurse recited a poem he had learnt,

Razors pain you, rivers are damp,
Acid stains you, pills cause cramp,
Guns aren't lawful, nooses give Gas smells

awful, you might as well live.
The routine on this ward was one of extreme caution and all new patients on admission had their clothes and belongings taken from them and searched. Suicidal patients had their shoe laces, ties, and belts removed and kept in dressing gowns and pyjamas, (without the cords).They used plastic cutlery and crockery, and the nurse had to make sure they swallowed their medication in their presence. The observation of some patients was very demanding so staff usually did it in one hour shifts.

Many of the patients were on active treatment programmes, and those able attended the occupational therapy department that was situated at the end of the ward. Here they did woodwork, painting and craft work. There was a general shortage of occupational therapists so a lot of their activities was in group work, such as reality orientation, quizzes and outside activities.

There were two long stay patients on the ward, who had their own side rooms. They worked in the kitchen and ward. They had been here many years and respected by the staff. In times of difficulty they had been known to assist the staff in quelling a violent episode, they were not expected to, they just did. I was warned however, to be careful what I said in their presence, and never forget that they were patients.

Chapter Eighteen.

Charlie sat on his bed and thought about what
the doctor had said to him. It seemed strange
to think about the things they had discussed.
He had settled down in the Bache Hall and
believed his future would be staying there. He
had heard that two of the patients were now
working in town in a hotel as kitchen porters,
and a woman had found employment in a cake
shop.
 A male nurse had been appointed to the role of
Employment officer, and it was he who would
decide how much incentive money would be
paid to each patient. As the rehabilitation
scheme had developed it had been necessary
for someone to co-ordinate the work available
within the hospital, but now it would be
expanded into the community.
The employment officer visited all the wards
and departments to ascertain how much work
was available in the hospital and to see what
that work entailed.
There was an ever increasing lobby, especially
from the patient welfare groups, about the role
of patients and the work they were expected to

do. A few said it was an exploitation of patients' rights and it was becoming more fashionable to change the term work to 'therapy'. Someone even compared the patients barrow gangs with the gangs seen in the American penal system.

Charlie, like most of the patients didn't care what they called it. To him it still meant getting up and going to his place of work each day. He was happy doing his ward work and, as the charge nurse on the ward had said, he didn't need the extra stress of doing anything else.

'One step as a time,' he said to Charlie... and most of the staff agreed with him. The charge nurse also had an opinion about what he called the

'do good brigade' and predicted that patients would become bored and apathetic if their work was stopped. He referred particularly to the long

term patient who wasn't chosen for the rehabilitation scheme. They could function satisfactory in the gang (team), under supervision, but left to their own desires they would just sit and smoke themselves to death.

He compared his 'do good brigade' to overseas missionaries who forced their Christian beliefs on the natives. They would believe in anything for a bowl of rice, just as some of the patients here would, for a cigarette.

Charlie was improving mentally and had started to read the magazines in the lounge. They were mainly women's magazines but he liked reading the agony aunt column and looking at the pictures of holiday destinations. Charlie cut some of the pictures out and taped them to his wall. His favourite was a mountain scene with peaks covered in snow, an ice blue lake and a little hut with a jetty nearby. He had never had a proper holiday but had once been on a school day trip to Wales. He had enjoyed it even though he had taken some stick from the other kids when it became known that his payment had been subsidised from the school funds.

One Saturday morning the staff were taking some of the 'rehab' patients to town, to buy some new clothes and Charlie was asked to join them.

Reluctantly, and after much persuasion he

accepted, so after lunch he was in the group that boarded the bus into town. They got off near the town hall and made their way to their first port of call, Burton's (the tailors). It was here, and in other shops the hospital had started a scheme where patients could be fitted out for new clothes, on account. The nurse from the ward would sign a chit, and once authorised by a senior nurse, patients could purchase goods from these shops. The clothes would be paid for by the hospital from the patients account.

Many long stay patients had thousands of pounds in these accounts, money which had accumulated over many years from allowances to which they had been entitled.

Charlie felt disorientated as he walked through the town. He became anxious, started sweating profusely and felt light headed. One of the nurses, a middle aged lady, noticed this and took his arm, telling him to take deep breaths. Charlie felt better with her holding his arm and was amazed how everything around him seemed to be so busy and noisy. The traffic was loud and everyone seemed to be rushing around.

They arrived in the shop and went upstairs to where the suits were on display. Charlie sat down on one of the few chairs available and looked around him while the nurse explained their mission to the staff. They seemed quite annoyed that they had turned up on a busy Saturday afternoon, but a young man was pleasant to the patients, when he found time to attend to them. Charlie looked at the clothes on display and was unhappy with what he saw. He had been admitted in what they had called fancy clothes, but here he could see pink coloured shoes, purple ties and suits with thin lapels, some buttoned up to the top of the chest.

The assistant showed them several modern styles, but Charlie decided to have a more conventional suit. He felt awkward and uneasy as the assistant measured him up; he was not used to people touching him and he certainly wasn't used to people calling him 'Sir'. In fact, it felt false and condescending, and it took all his will power for him to co-operate. It was hot and claustrophobic and his vest was wringing wet with sweat. He was glad to leave, but was told that he would have to return for a fitting.

After they had finished their shopping they went for a coffee in the 'Rows'. Charlie was amazed by what he saw... the coffee bar was painted in bright colours, had a jukebox on the wall, and the coffee was served from a machine that made a gurgling sound, and when it arrived it seemed to be all froth. It was noisy with bright lights glaring into his face and again he felt that unreal feeling coming on as the music banged away. He felt as if he was fading away... and then nothing.

He came around on the floor. He didn't know where he was and several faces were staring at him.

'Hello Charlie,' someone was saying as they smacked him lightly across the face.

He didn't know what had happened and hit out at the faces which seemed to surround him. There was a smashing noise as cups and saucers were falling from the table that Charlie was trying to climb up. He tried to heave himself up only to pass out again as the table fell on top of him.

When he woke up he was in a bed in the hospital's new sick ward which had replaced the one in the Annexe, where the beds had become blocked with elderly patients.

The patients here were mainly post operative, or physically ill. They were transferred from their wards so that they could receive specialised care.

The room Charlie was in had six bays. The doctor examined him and found there to be nothing seriously wrong, so after a routine forty eight hour period of observation he returned to the Bache hall. The doctor told him that he had suffered from a severe anxiety attack, and dehydration, the former probably caused from experiencing his first visit to town for several years.

Many of the staff lived in the nurses home.
Like the wards it was divided into separate
male and female sides, with a central
recreational room.

Chapter nineteen.

The day I was to take my final examinations
arrived with alarming speed.
I had tried to discipline myself to stay in after
work and study, but this was difficult as the
long summer evenings were a strong
distraction. After a long day in the ward or
classroom, it was easier to go for a walk or a
drink than study. I was already under pressure
with all our w edding arrangements to finalise
and found it difficult to concentrate on reading
a textbook.
My 'class' had spent the previous two weeks in
the training school preparing for the exams
and I studied as much as I could. But, like
everybody else, I was anxious and
apprehensive and we were all becoming
moody and intolerant towards each other.
The big day soon came and we hung around
the front door of the school of nursing,
smoking. Some were already making excuses
about why they would fail.
Personally, I began to regret the extra pressure
I had put on myself by deciding to get married
on the same day the results were due, but it

was too late to change the plans.

When the examination time approached we all rushed for a final visit to the toilet and then assembled in the classroom to wait for the examination papers to be distributed. We couldn't sit in our usual places as the desks had been rearranged, so I sat next to a wall where there would be less of a distraction.

The tutor came into the room, looking very serious, and distributed the exam papers. My heart was thumping as I read the questions carefully, as he had advised, then marked the ones I would attempt to answer.

The first question was about 'creating, and maintaining a therapeutic environment within a ward of long stay patients' and included a part on institutionalisation'.

The second was about depression, and the nursing care of a suicidal patient, and included different situations as to what parts of the Mental Health Act might be used.

The third question asked about Psychosomatic illnesses, the symptoms and the nursing care.

The next question was about the roles of certain professionals in the preparation and discharge of a Schizophrenic patient who had been in the hospital for most of his life, and included the different aspects of Care in the Community.

The final one was on Hysterical disorders and included a section on special syndromes, including anorexia nervosa, and hysterical pseudo-dementia.

After the exams some of the students had to go back on duty. Previously it had been customary for students to also be on duty before the exams. Fortunately, I was off duty so I went back to the nurse's home to commence the long six-week wait for the results....and my wedding. We had invited some of the other students to our wedding, and I hoped they would all pass. I could not imagine how we would feel if any of us didn't. I spent the next few weeks on the admission ward and was given more responsibility now that my exams were over. The charge nurse told me to start thinking like a staff nurse, and that the real learning had only just begun. If I passed I would have to learn how to teach others and to delegate. I was often sent to take charge of long stay wards, everything changed so quickly and I was treated as if I was qualified.

I began to learn new skills, such as report writing and ordering stock, and more importantly learning how to assess clinical situations and make accurate reports for the senior nursing and medical staff.

It was a strange time for me. The days before the wedding seemed to be approaching rapidly, and I was seeing my fiancé most nights to make sure everything was ready for our wedding. Yet the time to when the results came out seemed to drag on....it was weird.

I was becoming more stressed by the day, so spent a lot of time exercising in the gym or running along the canal. To help cover the expense of our wedding and moving into a flat I did as much overtime as I could get, so spent many 14 hour shifts on the ward.

One patient on the ward had been admitted with paralysis of the lower limbs and was confined to a wheelchair. It made me think about one of the questions from the exam. The history of his case was that he got himself into serious business and financial difficulties, and one day he found he had lost the use of his legs he couldn't get out of bed. He could not walk or move from the chair. Extensive medical tests had been unable to pinpoint the reason for his sudden paralysis, so he was referred to the psychiatrist. He was admitted to the ward as someone displaying 'Hysterical reaction, leading to paralysis'.

I knew about hysterical disorders. A certain type of behaviour and personality was said to be attributed to the condition, i.e. ill controlled outbursts of emotion seen in an immature personality. This behaviour could sometimes appear to be serving to manipulating a situation to the individual's advantage. The patient is unable to control the symptoms, in contrast to 'malingering' which is the conscious production of symptoms to achieve gain.

This particular patient seemed to have no interest in his personal situation. He was visited regularly by his worried relatives and had to be lifted in and out of a chair to meet with them. Despite his paralysis, he would cheerfully sit with his family and often make jokes with the staff. His appetite was good and he slept fairly well.

A test carried out with a needle showed that,

up to a point that ran in a straight line across his limbs, he had no feelings in his legs. The feelings did not follow the expected path which the nerves ran along and was known as the 'glove and stocking' distribution. There had been cases of blindness, amnesia, and loss of function of the limbs, all attributed to this condition.

Special syndromes also came under the heading of hysterical disorder such as, anorexia nervosa, and regression to childhood states. I was told that the patients would improve if the circumstances that were said to have caused it were to disappear.

Psychotherapy was discussed as an option. The nurses on the ward were told that a balance had to be struck between sympathy and firmness. Too much sympathy ran the risk of further hysterical symptoms, while to be over strict would lead to non co-operation and resistance to treatment. It was difficult to find the right balance as the patient was over friendly, demanding our attention by giving us the sweets and chocolate his frantic wife was bringing him each day. She did not understand why he was in a mental hospital and found it difficult to accept what she was told. She thought we were saying that he was malingering and that made her angry with him. She appeared close to a breakdown herself with the worry of her husband and their failing business.

Away from work, there was only a week to our big day. We had moved our belongings to our new flat, which was really a bedsitter and kitchen with shared toilet facilities. Although not ideal it was acceptable as it was difficult to find accommodation in town.

*****

Charlie moved back to the rehabilitation unit and once in the privacy of his own room and surrounded by his precious possessions he began to feel secure again. Charlie saw Dr Malstead, and was told to take a couple of days off work to convalesce. This pleased him because although he felt better sitting in his room, he felt uncomfortable when mixing or talking to others. He had difficulty in rationalising what had happened to him and this led to more feelings of anxiety. When asked, he couldn't tell anyone what had happened because he didn't know himself, though the nurses, meaning to reassure him, said that it was only an acute anxiety attack, and not something serious, such as a bad heart. Unfortunately, Charlie missed the point and felt that they meant he was making a fuss over nothing.

Following lots of T.L.C. (tender loving care) from his now favourite nurse, the one who had been in town with him, he began to improve and was soon ready to return to work.

Charlie had noticed that when he was seeing his patients, Dr Malstead talked to the staff, as though he was teaching them.

'What's the difference between convalescence and rehabilitation?' he asked them during a consultation with Charlie. One or two had given their versions, defining convalescence as a 'gradual recovery of health and strength after sickness', while rehabilitation involved the 'restoration of a handicapped person to the higher physical, mental, social, vocational and economic levels of which they are capable.' Charlie was in need of both. The doctor said he was not to be rushed into going out, but should be encouraged to attend hospital functions, the local shops and, perhaps, start going to the local pub at the end of the road for a snack and a drink.

He also remarked that patients were not to be regarded as being a success just because they were working in the hospital whilst on the rehabilitation scheme. They had to go further than work experience and be directed towards providing patients with a full and meaningful life again. It was down to the staff to follow the patients into the community and support and monitor their progress.

There was delight from the team when Dr Malstead announced that he had received funding to appoint a nurse, at sister grade, to take up this role.

A C.P.N. Community psychiatric nurse, responsible for newly discharged patients from the rehab' scheme.

Charlie got over his relapse in town and continued to improve mentally. He held down his job on the ward ans was practically regarded as one of the staff. His imput on the ward was becoming increasingly invaluable and, if he had a rare day off, his presence was missed. He was even having his tea break with the staff and found himself listening to gossip. Sometimes they forgot he was there and spoke about confidential and personal matters.

Not all the staff were happy with the situation and claimed that such liberties added to the grandiose ideas that Charlie had of himself. He took little notice; he had become the charge nurse's 'blue eye' and knew when it was acceptable for him to sit with them.

He was clever enough to talk to the charge nurse about his interest in horse racing. 'Are you having a bet today, boss?' he would ask, knowing that a response was guaranteed. Besides the charge nurse loved being called 'boss'.

He often asked Charlie which horses he fancied and before long it would become a two-way conversation with the rest of those present being ignored.

'You can put my bet on today, Charlie, you're my lucky mascot,' The charge nurse had said. Charlie was now feeling the benefits of being on the rehabilitation scheme. Living in his room was not much different to the staff living in their small rooms in the nurses home. They had the same facilities with shared baths and toilets, television lounge and meals served at set times.

Twice a week he was allowed to go for a pint after tea, and he had managed to return to town to collect his suit. He was still a young man and was thought of as one of the schemes stars, although there was still some concern about his paranoia.

The scheme was proving a success, and several patients were holding down jobs in the community. There were now 30 patients in Bache Hall and this had helped relieve some of the overcrowding on the wards.

Meanwhile, a major change occurred and it was to have a significant influence on Charlie's future. The hospital provided a budget for 'ward orderlies', to undertake non nursing duties on the long stay wards and, after long and intense deliberations between the rehabilitation team, management and the unions it was decided that some of the patients might be suitable. The job description was certainly not much different to what Charlie, and some of the other patients were now doing.

Suitable patients undertaking the work would be assessed over a three month period, and if they proved satisfactory they would be given the job on a permanent basis and become members of staff.

There was a cry of outrage and disbelief from some of the staff and all kind of threats were made about not working with them. Others argued that if they could not accept the successful rehabilitation of a mental patient, which meant giving them a job, how could they expect other agencies to do so. This forceful argument eventually won the day. Charlie's first reaction to the proposition was one of shock and disbelief. He was opposed to the idea as were some of the staff and he became anxious and fearful.

'Forget about it, just carry on doing your job,' his favourite nurse had advised him. He had tried to, but there was already some reaction from the staff on his ward and it was making him feel uncomfortable. The charge nurse told him that whether he was a patient or a member of staff, he wanted Charlie to continue working for him.

However, the seed had been planted in his mind and each night he lay on his bed turning over the idea in his mind of being on the staff. The more he thought about it, the more he could see himself in that role even though it frightened him. I'll show them, he told himself one night.

A further stroke of luck was a decision made that any patients employed could also move into the staff home, and until they had settled down they could still go to the Bache Hall for their meals and to receive their medication.

*****

Charlie looked out of the window of the room he had been given in the staff home. His favourite nurse had helped him move in, and settle down.

'What's it coming to when patients are moving in with us?' he had heard someone mutter when he moved in...and very soon a neighbour had banged on the wall to tell him to turn his radio down.

His room, above the main entrance was on the

third floor and he could see everyone coming and going. It was smaller than his room at Bache Hall and the toilet was along way down the corridor, which was a great inconvienience at night... it was also very noisy. He had been accustomed to all the patients being in bed by 10pm at the Bache Hall, but here they were coming in at all hours of the night, talking and laughing, and then banging their doors shut. He was very lonely and unhappy and felt almost as isolated as the day he was admitted. He had not really applied for the job. There had been a chat with the consultant, and then an assistant chief male nurse had visited him. 'Well done Charlie, you have done very well,' he had said.

Charlie told them that he didn't want to be on the staff, or move from his room, but they would have none of it. The scheme, they said depended on him and others like him to succeed, and that he could not be a patient for ever. There was a promise of support and he was persuaded to give it a try for the sake of others!

His favourite nurse had even promised to keep his room at Bache Hall empty for him and, eventually, he had relented. He signed the contract informing him of his starting pay and holidays.

Not a very important member of staff, he thought as he sat on his bed. They were now charging him for meals and his room, so he didn't have much more money than he had earned as a patient. In fact as he had not been properly discharged, he was still a patient. They had told him that he was an out patient and would still need to see the doctor and nurse to monitor his progress while the employment officer would provide support. He was too anxious to use the facilities in the staff home, or mix with the other residents, so most of the time he stayed in his room, lying on the bed. He even went to work on his day off, to relieve the boredom. He would sit in his kitchen chair and, with a brew of tea, read the paper behind the kitchen door. As long as he kept the kitchen clean, nobody minded, there was no relief on his day off so they were glad of his help. None of the nurses thought of him as a member of staff anyway. He was still treated as Charlie, the wards kitchen man, who did what he was told.

Lying there he fidgeted with a wooden coat
hanger he had found in the wardrobe. It had
S.M. written on it in blue ink. He wondered
what that stood for, and who had been in this
room before him.

*****

My big day came and I woke up with a
headache, as I had been out for a drink with
some of my mates, and had not got in until the
middle of the night. It's funny how you plan to
be in bed early, until you've had a drink and
then regardless of how important the following
day's event may be, you are persuaded to stay
out.
After a quick breakfast and a couple of
Aspirins, I eventually got into the bathroom to
get ready. I put on my suit, and was glad when
Bill arrived, he was my only colleague who
owned a reliable car and had offered to drive
me to church.
We got to the wedding later than we planned
as I couldn't remember the way, or the name of
the village. Nobody seemed to understand us

when we asked for St James' Church, in a
place we called 'Ros do' (Rhosddu)!
Eventually, we did arrive and as I walked up
the aisle I felt slightly embarrassed with my
freshly cut hair and brand new suit. I paused to
whisper to some of my colleagues, to find out
if they had passed their finals.
The organ suddenly sprang into life and the
wedding ceremony began. Up she walked, the
girl who was to become my wife, looking
radiant and beautiful in her wedding gown. At
last the waiting was over. Everything went
smoothly as we sang the hymns and made our
vows. We even looked into each other's eyes as
we said, 'I do'.
Later I sat at the reception and picked up the
place card which said
'bridegroom' and I wrote underneath,
S.Murphy, R.M.N. (Registered Mental Nurse).
It was the happiest day of my life. We were
married and now I was a Qualified nurse.

A lament for the Asylum.

And now it's gone, a community that survived
with little contact with the outside world,
self sufficient, with its farms and shops.
Jobs passed down, with each generation,
like the madness they served,
a hereditary thing, to pass on and marry
within.

Even the chimney was reduced in size
as if too majestic to serve its empire,
an empire that grew, to protect the vulnerable,
the meek, the wild, the ones society locked
away.
Out of sight, out of mind, only to resurface,
when society cried,
the community cares, 'Let them out'.

And once out, they went back to their apathy,
their conscience clear, a deed well done.
So out they are, lonely and vulnerable,
sleeping in boxes, without shoes or socks,
confused by society's reaction and
indifference,
while the cosy asylum rots away. S
S.M.

I commenced my nursing career in 1959 as a
cadet nurse at the Deva hospital, Chester, and
retired in 1997. Twelve weeks later I returned
as a part time staff nurse to work in the
electro-convulsive therapy unit. During my
career I qualified as a Registered Mental
Nurse, and then trained at the Chester Royal
Infirmary and City Hospital, to become a State

Registered Nurse. For twenty years I was employed as a senior nurse manager, and completed fifty years service in the Nursing profession.

Since 1829, when an asylum was built, the mentally ill have been nursed on the site of the Countess of Chester Health Park. Today they are cared for in a new purpose built unit known as Bowmere hospital.

At its peak, the asylum housed 1,800 beds and patients were admitted from an area extending from Birkenhead to Northwich.

Since the early 1960's there has been a steady reduction in the number of beds within mental hospitals, both locally and nationally, and the old asylums have been demolished or upgraded for other usages.

Although fictitious, my story is based on fact. Some of the events that occurred at the hospital, such as the major fire in the main hall (Sunday March 7th, 1971) did occur. I have changed the dates to fit into Charlie's story, a patient whom I knew extremely well.

Acknowledgement.
I am indebted to Mark Bevan, of Cheshire Country Publishing, without whose guidance and experience this, and my other books may not have been published.

Books by Stan Murphy
    available from Amazon e-books.

The Best is yet to be.

The Doctor, the Dictionary, and the Deva.

The Deva Despatch.

Upton and Newton at the Cheshire Show.

Every Picture tells a story.

The attendant and His Handbook,
(night duty in the asylum).

The Looney Minder, (Rhyme, reason and
tripolar disorder).

Blacons Airmen. (Blacon Cemetery).

The final Curtain, (memories from Chester's
Mental Hospital).

A Century of Influenza and Viruses.

I'm The only Celebrity Here,
(Gwryth Castle, Abergele).

Who switched the Lights On.
(Blackpool Illuminations).

The Birds Food Bank.
(Children's Story).

The Word, (Book series).

Printed in Great Britain
by Amazon

85825634R00190